SHADOW OF WHIMSY

A CAPE COD LOVE STORY

ANN HYMES

SHADOW OF WHIMSY

For information about this title, contact the publisher:
Secant Publishing, LLC
P.O. Box 79
Salisbury MD 21803

www.secantpublishing.com

ISBN 978-1-944962-13-5 (hardcover)
ISBN 978-1-944962-15-9 (paperback)

Library of Congress Control Number: 2016937927

Printed in the United States of America
Design by: Kit Foster Design

For June Beckman

CHAPTER ONE

Theresa Alston Crandall wondered whether going away for awhile would help her focus on her marriage or allow it to die from neglect. She was thirty-four years old. Her marriage was a mess, a tangle of boredom and predictability, wrapped like a package that she dangled over a cliff. She couldn't let go, and she didn't know how to hold on. She felt separate from the life she had created. Elusive aspects of her family's past were taking shape in the form of a faraway inheritance: a house named Whimsy Towers.

She'd spent the past five months meeting with lawyers and probate officers to get to this moment, and she was heading off on an adventure to see a house that was shrouded in secrets. Her husband wanted her to wait until he could take vacation time and go with her, but Theresa felt the need to meet the ghosts of her family's past on her own. She and their dog would drive to Cape Cod and spend a couple of weeks at Whimsy Towers. She looked forward to having time alone far from her familiar life, to finding out whether distraction was a form of progress or merely pretending.

Buying a new car would help sink fresh footprints in the future. In the local Volvo showroom, a car salesman, dressed in a loose dark suit with copious creases and speaking too softly, was trying to keep her attention. His sales pitch sounded like a recording from a seminar. He talked and did not listen. Theresa wasn't interested in the mechanics of a car and simply wanted dependability and storage capacity for the trip ahead. She stared at a large stain on the man's necktie as he rambled on. The greasy smear on the tie covered the rear legs of a moose standing next to a spindly pine tree. Almost caught in the loose knot at his open collar, a faded full moon cast eerie light on the moose antlers. The man was perspiring. He tapped a clipboard against his thigh and then ran the tips of his fingers across his moist temple, fidgeting and glancing repeatedly over his shoulder.

Theresa wondered whether he was married. *Could a man get past his wife wearing a greasy moose tie?* She smiled at the thought of Kevin wearing a tie with a moose on it. He picked all his own clothes, and a really daring tie would be wide stripes instead of narrow. They had been married almost twelve years, and she had never seen so much as a crumb on his tie.

"Excuse me, ma'am. I'm not sure you heard me say about the injectors. This new fueling system will deliver maximum torque to the drive wheels, and the double overhead cams make for very smooth acceleration. Would you like to, uh, take a test drive?" He paused. "Or shall we wait for your husband?"

The salesman's remark jolted Theresa from her absent musings about Kevin. *Wait for your husband.* She repeated his words several times in her head. He was leaning toward her through the open car window as she sat in the driver's seat. She stretched her arms straight out and turned her wrists slightly to feel the wheel go right and left. The car was perfect. It had the highest safety rating of all station wagons, and she felt good just sitting in it. She had come to buy this specific car in the showroom, and, no, she didn't even need to drive it. And especially, no, she didn't need her husband to make a decision.

"My husband?" Her neck stiffened, and she felt the weight of a million women who made decisions only at the pleasure of their husbands, or made no decisions at all. She was leaving that life behind, and this car was to take her to a place she'd never been and an inheritance she didn't understand. And now a man with a greasy moose had reminded her that there would always be stones in the path of new beginnings.

"I just mean ..." he said uncomfortably. "I thought . . ." He started to straighten and pull back from the window. Theresa felt trapped and smothered. The car now felt like a cage, giving this awkward, perspiring man control over her. She reached out toward him and grabbed his necktie at the greasy moose legs, pulling his face back through the window. His clipboard hit the floor, and his hands spread out on the side of the car as if to brace him from being pulled in on top of her.

"You thought! You thought what?" she nearly screamed, startled by her own strength, but still not letting go. "You thought a woman with a wedding ring couldn't come in here and buy a car? Well, I've got news for you. I came here to write a check for this car. This car! My check, my car!"

His face was just inches from hers. His eyebrows had disappeared under the hair that fell forward, and his mouth gaped, revealing stained teeth. His breath was nasty. Theresa was disgusted, both with him and with the realization that women in 1980 still had to fight their way up the ladder of choices.

Releasing her grip on the salesman's tie, Theresa watched him stumble backwards as she opened the door and got out. He caught his balance and ran shaky fingers through his hair but did not bend to retrieve the clipboard. His eyes stayed focused on her. Two other men came toward them from across the room, one almost running and one with more measured pace. A woman stood up from behind a potted palm. Theresa slammed the car door behind her and headed for the showroom exit. She was aware of voices and footsteps, but she never looked back.

Her knees felt weak but seemed to carry her forward with determination. With long strides, she crossed the parking lot quickly and reached her old Volvo. Before opening the door, she stopped to take a deep breath and held her hands out in front of her, palms up. The hand that had grabbed the necktie was shaking. Curving her fingertips into the soft palm, she rubbed them gently and then made a fist, feeling the sensation of something greasy. Perhaps it was her imagination.

Hurriedly, Theresa started the car. She had wanted a

newer model for the long trip that lay ahead of her, but as she moved through the gears, she relaxed with the comfort of its familiar feel. The worn leather seat fit her perfectly. Her favorite radio stations were preset, and the mirrors were at just the right levels. Sometimes the sunroof got stuck in the open position, but since they had a garage, it didn't bother her. Kevin lost patience with the unreliable cruise control, but Theresa never noticed.

She and this car had a history together. Over 200,000 miles provided lots of opportunity for bonding. She knew its lines by heart and could park it in spaces considered hopeless by others. The forest green paint still waxed up pretty well, even with little hints of rust at the rear bumper. And it was not just a fair-weather friend; it was a workhorse car.

Their dog loved to go for rides, leaving yellow hair everywhere and willingly moving over to accommodate loads of azalea bushes or tomato cages. More than once, Theresa had arrived home with a piece of antique furniture squeezed into the back or hanging out the rear with a little red flag—like the Chinese headboard with delicately carved golden dragons and kissing birds.

And the baby crib and rocker. Theresa's eyes began to fill with tears as she remembered the beautiful autumn day she and Kevin had found just the furniture they wanted for the baby. Their precious baby. The tears rolled down her cheeks, falling in damp streaks on her silk blouse. She wondered what had happened to the never-used furniture. Perhaps Kevin had quietly given it away or had stored it like family heirlooms that wait in dark places.

They had wanted a large family, a picket fence, and a dog. Kevin worked hard to provide for his wife, focusing on goals. He was conscientious and smart, but Theresa got lost in the disappointment of dreams. She was hungry for life, for passion, for tomorrows that did not duplicate today. What had materialized was a dog. She loved her husband but wondered whether there was a compelling future for them. She yearned for love that was behavior, not a feeling. *What is enough? And when are dreams just the postponement of living?*

Caught in the easy rhythm of the familiar drive and her wandering thoughts, Theresa almost didn't notice the Jeep dealership. She passed it every day, but today she suddenly turned sharply to catch the drive leading to the sales lot. A row of four-door models was carefully arranged in a straight line, with balloons bobbing wildly in the wind. Mentally she began matching the colors of the balloons with the car colors: two reds, green, white, a dark blue.

"May I help you?" said a voice, accompanied by a tapping on her front passenger window. "Care to take a look? They're just in."

"Oh," replied Theresa, startled. A young man was coming around in front of her car to her side, and she stepped out to meet him. "Red and six cylinders," she said.

"Excuse me?"

"Red and six cylinders. And leather seats would be nice. If you've got one, I'll take it."

The young man gave her a look of disbelief and then headed straight to the row of cars and the window stickers on the two red ones. "Take your pick," he called triumphantly. "They're exactly the same, except one has a CD player."

She nodded, walking toward him. "I'll take that one. And don't tell me a word about cams and injectors and RPMs. Does it have power windows?"

"Yes, ma'am."

"Well then, write it up. I'll come back to pick up the Volvo."

"Yes, ma'am." The young man clumsily handed her a business card with one hand and tried to tuck in his shirt with the other. He stumbled toward the car door, gathering dust on his shiny black shoes. Theresa wondered whether he had just made his first sale. She wanted to ask him his age. *Did he like his job?* He made her feel strangely old. She watched the boyish face as he drove her red Jeep toward the sales office.

The gap in the row of cars gave her an odd feeling. She imagined all the Jeeps driving in unison to this spot, in tightly-spaced formation, headlights perfectly aligned. They were a unit, and breaking rank from the group disrupted the harmony of the line. Stepping out broke the order, the pact; places had to be reassigned.

Without consciously deciding to do it, Theresa stepped into the space vacated by her new Jeep. She was not used to change. The routine of her marriage and daily life provided safety from the unexpected, like a familiar rut that deepens gradually. She felt dried tears tingling on her face as she glanced at the vehicles on each side being left behind. In a soft voice, she whispered, "Sorry, Kevin." A few weeks apart would test her marriage, her commitment, and her desire for independence.

The eager young salesman interrupted her mood. "The paperwork will take a few minutes. Would you like to come in and sit down?"

"No," she replied, digging her fingernails into her palms. "I'd like to wash my hands."

ගෂ

A twist of fate had brought Theresa Crandall as a child to Virginia. The family had no roots there. She and her father were her whole family. Her earliest memories were of people towering over her and the sounds of parades in the street. She could still feel her father's hand tight around hers as he led her through noisy crowds of schoolchildren, bagpipers, and sweaty vendors hawking hot pretzels. It was always sunny.

When he lifted her to his shoulders, she could see the marching bands and decorated cars with smiling people who waved and threw candy that bounced onto the sidewalk. As rows of drummers came into view, Theresa would straighten her back and tap enthusiastically on the smooth bald spot on her father's head, but he never complained. Unlike Kevin, who worried about percentage of body fat and his first few gray hairs, her father lived a life of quiet acceptance and balance. He seemed beyond the reach of vanity and didn't fret over the look of things. For years he sat alone in the bleachers during Theresa's early morning practice sessions before school at the indoor ice rink near their home. With rumpled hair and nearly matching clothes, he huddled over coffee, watching her turn slowly and carefully on one foot as she made precise concentric circles. It was hard work for a child. The blade edges of a dozen young skaters scratched into the ice, cutting the sleepy silence of the rink. They glided and turned, each in a separate marked patch, learning to respect the boundaries of others.

Theresa's hair was dark and curly, not at all like her father's sandy blond color. She had kept it short for skating and never let it grow. Kevin didn't comment on her appearance or the way she wore her hair. He seemed to accept her the way one moves past colorful wallpaper that is not changed over time. It settles in. The invisible details of who she was had accumulated over the years. Once she almost asked the hairdresser to spike her bangs and dye them green for St. Patrick's Day, but she didn't think Kevin would be amused. Just the thought of surprise on his face made her laugh; she didn't need to do it.

Her father had always been her best friend, a talented writer and patient mentor, the potter's hand that gently shaped her life. He was quiet and caring. She was an only child whose constant playmate was an imagination that carried her through doors not opened; they traveled effortlessly together. Her father tried to support these flights of fantasy and inquiry, except for one.

Her mother.

It was hard to get enough pieces of the puzzle to have more than a hint of the whole. Theresa hoped her upcoming trip to Whimsy Towers would answer questions about family revelations that had come to light since her father's recent death. She knew little about her maternal grandmother, not to mention her house in Cape Cod, and would have to retrace her family's steps to fill in the story. Probate lawyers deal in facts, without emotion, and they had prompted her decision to tease the present with the past. She was anxious to get started. Her father had held parts of her life that should have been given to her. *Why had he told her so little about her grandmother? And what was the truth of her mother's death?* As a child, Theresa was told only that her mother had "gone on," that she was happy but would not be coming home. The concept of death was like a long vacation, but Theresa could not go visit. Once she had packed her tiny suitcase, hoping.

Eventually, as an adult, she learned from her father that Emily, her mother, had been raised in South Carolina and Massachusetts, but there were few details—and no photographs.

CHAPTER TWO

Theresa pulled up to the house and parked her shiny new red car in the garage, happy with the final outcome of a bumpy morning.

"Hi Kevin, I'm home," she called, tossing the keys to the Jeep on the hall table.

"Did you find something?" he answered from the den.

"Sure did. Want to see it?"

There was a pause. "See it? Are you on a test drive?"

Kevin appeared at the door of the den, meeting Theresa as she turned the corner.

"No, I bought it. I bought a Jeep."

Kevin's jaw dropped. He looked as though someone had hit a fly ball just over his head, and he couldn't quite reach it. "You've already bought a car?" he stammered, gripping the papers that were slipping out of his hand.

"Yup."

"I thought you were going to look at a station wagon for the trip."

"I was, but that didn't work out," she replied, able now to smile at the thought of the commotion she'd caused in the showroom. "Come on, I'll take you for a ride. Let's get a strawberry milkshake at Bob's to celebrate. Where's the dog?"

Theresa kept moving down the hall, alternately whistling and calling, "Gypsy! Here, girl!"

The house was bigger than they needed for the two of them. They avoided the subject of moving, the mention of change. It was easier just to keep their lives going in familiar surroundings, filling up the extra rooms, exchanging barrenness for possessions. Spaces were filled comfortably with the illusion of home. Neither wanted to move memories from the rooms that held them for fear of losing the desire to make new ones. Their marriage seemed on hold, waiting for the spark that would rekindle it. The delicate truce that kept each of them from letting go and admitting failure also kept them grasping at the hope of possibilities just around the corner. Theresa sensed that Whimsy Towers might upset that fragile balance.

She saw Kevin standing in the doorway, trying to process the last thirty seconds. She knew he often didn't understand his wife or what she did. He tried, but he was wired for order and analysis. Buying a car in less than an hour and wanting a milkshake at 10:30 on Saturday morning would make no sense to him. He tightened his hold on the papers in his hand, waiting, searching for a hint of logic in what was going on.

But Theresa didn't easily bow to logic, and she reappeared with their yellow Labrador, who was obviously roused from slumber but ready for an outing. Kevin would need to catch up or miss the moment. Theresa playfully caught his sleeve as she passed him, giving it a tug. "Come on, you're going to love it. Honest."

The dog didn't hesitate to jump into the new car, eagerly positioning herself in the middle of the back seat, sitting up tall like a trusted sentinel. Theresa slid in behind the wheel and adjusted the already-adjusted mirror. Kevin followed and got in the passenger side, pulling the door closed with a look of surprised satisfaction. "Feels nice." He smiled and put his hand on her thigh, patting and rubbing her gently. Theresa felt a warm sensation. She loved his touch at unexpected times. She knew he loved her, desired her, but often was wrapped too tightly in the demands of work and responsibility. Sexual intimacy was a category in their life that increasingly had a scheduled time and place. *Lawyers need patterns.*

Theresa did not start the car. She leaned over toward him, and his hand moved deeper between her legs. She felt moist and eager. They began kissing, and she climbed over onto his lap. Unlike guilty teenagers fumbling in the back seat, they swiftly accommodated the limited space on the passenger side, rising to the moment of unplanned pleasure. Desire and opportunity came together on the soft leather seat of a car with steamed windows. Kevin wrapped his wife in his arms and seemed to accept the illogic of the situation in silence. He looked happy and relaxed and continued to caress Theresa. She made no effort to move off him. Gypsy stretched out in the back, comfortable and patient.

"See, I knew you'd like it," Theresa said softly.

"And we are talking about the car?"

They kissed again, and Theresa felt a fresh closeness

to this man who didn't often show kinks in his armor.

"So you think I did okay?" she asked, throwing him a teasing grin as she climbed back behind the wheel.

"This car has magic properties, Theresa, and it's been christened in a most wonderful way. If you like it, I'm happy, but I can remember when your idea of impulse buying was a pair of new earrings!"

She kissed him affectionately on the cheek. "The mileage isn't great, but it's just right for hauling the stuff I want to take up to the Cape."

Kevin took a minute to respond. "You know that change is hard for me, pushing me out of my comfort zone. I want to support you, to understand you, Theresa, but surprises throw me off. I do love you so much, even with all the crazy ideas that scare me. And now I have the feeling your grandmother's inheritance will change our lives, and I don't want to lose you."

They looked at each other, but no more was said on the subject. Boundaries were being tested before new rules were in place. The future was drawing a circle around the present that might not hold it.

ᘓ

Early the following Saturday, Kevin helped load the new car for the trip north. The middle of May is beautiful in northern Virginia. Bright tulips were still blooming along the side of the driveway, and the irises would soon open. Theresa had planted dozens of daffodils and irises near the oak trees in their yard. She had brought the bulbs from her father's house, the home she'd grown up in, just a few blocks away. Their dog was well beyond her digging days, and the flowers grew tall and undisturbed. Theresa would miss seeing the spiked clusters of purple and peach irises burst into color this year. The trip ahead was pulling her from what was familiar and safe, and she felt unsettled, apprehensive.

"Kevin, do you think if I cut some iris stems and kept them in water, they would bloom in Cape Cod?"

"I don't think the blossoms are set enough, never mind the thought of a vase of water jiggling around in your new car."

"I know," she sighed. "It's just that I love these flowers, and they remind me of my father. They'll be opening without me."

She, too, was blooming without her father, going on without him, and there was no reversing nature's course. Since his death at Christmas, he had been in her thoughts even more than when he was alive. They had been so close, seeing each other almost every day; but with his passing, Theresa had learned things that colored the memories. *Had she been protected from the past or denied its relevance?* She yearned to talk with him, to ask questions, but it was too late, and all the other voices were silent. She hoped that Whimsy Towers could shed light on the family history. *Was she wise to want to unmask the dark spaces?*

Kevin left her with her thoughts. She wondered

whether digging into the past would alter her feelings for her father. He and Kevin, too, had been close, often watching football or sharing tips on lawn care and stock market swings. Her father had graciously released his only child and the light of his life to the care of a husband, a young lawyer with a bright future and serious plans. Theresa loved the two men in her life.

"Should I take some blankets?" she called down to the driveway from the bedroom window. "The house is furnished, but I don't know about extra things. What do you think about pots and pans?"

Kevin was pushing a large clay pot of herbs into the back of the car, wedging it between the beach chair and a huge basket of paperback books. "I think blankets are a good idea. It's probably still cool there, especially at night. Forget kitchen stuff, though; you can pick up whatever you need." He paused and laughed. "Are you planning to open a library?"

Theresa wasn't sure how to pack for a trip alone. Kevin would never haul a pot of herbs and two hanging baskets of pink petunias on a ten-hour drive, but he knew better than to question. What was reasonable to Theresa often did not register in the same way with Kevin. They had come to accept that some subjects were not worth discussing between them; the differing point of view was so certain that it would only cause hurt or stress, and neither could see the other's side. Sometimes it was better to let go and move on, pretending there was peace.

Theresa was still upstairs, sitting on the end of their

bed. Her purse, her feather pillow, and a large straw hat with a sunflower stitched on the front lay next to her. She glanced down at her suitcases, a gift from her father when she graduated from high school. They had accompanied her the first time she had ever been away from him. Although the University of Virginia was only a couple of hours from home, the separation had been hard for them both. Each was all the family the other had. Now she was leaving behind another man who loved her and from whom she was not used to being separated. She told herself that two weeks was just enough to settle her questions and return. *Can you wear out a marriage like a pair of favorite shoes?* She wanted clarity, and distance was a tempting companion to escape a relationship that was suffocating.

When her father had become ill shortly before the holidays, Theresa had watched him withdraw more and more into himself. He had rarely left his house, and if she and Kevin hadn't tended to the snow, checked on bills, and made sure he had groceries, her father might have succeeded in becoming a model hermit. His death left her with a modest estate: his small house with its attic of things to go through, a collection of baseball cards, and a metal box of important papers. It was in this box she found the letter that would alter the future.

For at least the hundredth time, Theresa took the letter from her purse, carefully unfolded it, and began to read the familiar handwriting.

My dearest Theresa,

I cannot leave you without telling you some things you have long wondered about. I do not easily revisit these details of my past, but I understand your hunger for them, and I will try to share memories that I have wanted to hide even from myself.

Do you remember years ago when we used to walk to the park and look up into the sky at the stars? You would ask me if Mommy could see the stars. I always told you that she could see everything that was beautiful and that you were her favorite star. Your mother was so full of life and love. She saw only good in everyone she met, and her contagious joy touched all who knew her. When she was gone, my heart went to that faraway place with her, unable to be separated. Seeing so much of her in you has brightened all the stars of heaven for me.

When we were married, your grandmother, Theodosia Hampton, was living in Cape Cod, Massachusetts, apart from her husband. As the beautiful young bride of a wealthy, older man, she had felt stifled by life in the South Carolina Lowcountry and took off for Paris in the 1920s. She came back pregnant and madly in love with a famous, and married, Left Bank artist. Her unhappy husband was an important attorney from a prominent family, and an elaborate tale was fabricated to ward off scandal. The child born to them was your mother.

Your grandparents kept the appearance of a marriage, but a loveless understanding was the bargain they struck. Boarding school and shuffling between South Carolina and the Cape were the requirements of Emily's childhood. The-

odosia adored her only child, treasuring the time together, teaching her to ride and sail, to paint and recite poetry. The Cape Cod house brimmed with laughter and visitors, good food and conversation. Where Theodosia was, there was vitality.

We lived happily in that house when you were a baby, until the storm came that changed everything. Clouds descended and hid the sun. Our patterns of contentment were shattered, and the road split without goodbyes.

Storms are not uncommon off the coast of Cape Cod. Winds howl up the rugged coast, gathering trees and chunks of shoreline in their erratic dance of power. Nature has the last word on who or what survives its whims, and your mother loved the challenge of the contest.

Late September is an exciting time for sailing. The summer residents are gone, and the open sea churns with shifts in current and wind. Your mother could not resist racing with the wild, daring the sails to pull her across the breaking waves. The sea spray, the lunging boat with straining keel pounding through the water, and the prospect of a day without destination were thrilling to her.

But the storm was the winner the afternoon she did not come back. An offshore hurricane made an unexpected turn toward land. The skies darkened quickly with a sickening purple haze, and the wind shrieked between bolts of lightning that lit up an angry, swirling ocean. I came home early from the office and searched and waited. Theodosia held you close and read stories until you finally fell asleep in her protective arms. Bits of the boat were eventually found, *but that was all.*

As the days and weeks passed, your grandmother began to hallucinate and call out to her missing daughter, warning her not to go sailing. I could no longer trust her to care for you, and I could not stay where I, too, was haunted by images at every turn. A nurse came to live with Theodosia, and I left my beloved wife in the bosom of the ocean she loved so much. She was two months pregnant with our next baby.

Theresa, I am sorry not to have told you these things before. It seemed best for you to believe that all your grandparents were dead, but Theodosia died only four years ago. I have not seen her since the day I left with you. Her mind slowly slipped away, and she recognized no one. She was well cared for, and you were my future. It was too painful to look back.

Theodosia rewrote her will as soon as we left, leaving her estate and home to you, her only heir, with the provision that it not pass to you until my death. Local bank trustees have cared for it these last years. I know you will love Whimsy Towers. Its walls have witnessed passion and hope and the dramas of extraordinary lives.

My only request, dear Theresa, is that you take my ashes back to Cape Cod and scatter them in the ocean, where they will join your mother and unborn brother or sister in the cool, deep currents. And when you see the stars in the vast skies over the Atlantic Ocean, remember there are two hearts cherishing you.

I love you, Dad

Theresa refolded the letter and repeated the last words to herself: "... remember there are two hearts cherishing you." *Two hearts. The love of parents, the unconditional caring and commitment that binds generations and expectation.* When she had come home from college and announced that Kevin had asked her to marry him, her father had seen her happiness and asked only one question: "Does he cherish you?"

The question had startled her, and she had not been able to answer. Kevin was thoughtful and bright; he was so earnest. He avoided the endless drunken college revelries and macho contests. He was serious about his studies and took only courses that challenged him. She loved being with him and making him laugh. Education and law were the pathway to the future for Kevin, but with very few stops along the way for diversion. He was grounded; she fluttered. *She did not consider that being solid might also be boring.*

They had met in a senior seminar called "Shakespeare and the Male Ego." Theresa spoke up in class and was full of questions and ideas; he was quiet and observing. She had curiosity and conviction and was opening her wings for flight.

"Do you think Macbeth ever loved his wife?" she asked the professor, but looking at her fellow students. "Could they ever trust each other?"

A lively discussion ensued about the threats to fidelity and the dangers of intimacy. Theresa wanted to explore the emotions of relationships and understand how people connected. She was not afraid to probe, but she listened respectfully to the assumptions of others. Kevin did not often speak up, but she felt him watching her, and she liked it.

One day at the end of class, as students were leaving the room, Theresa turned to him and asked unexpectedly, "What made you take this course, Kevin?"

They had not had any direct, personal conversation, and he stopped packing up his books in order to answer. "I'm headed to law school, and I figure a good lawyer needs to understand Hamlet, Richard III, and Macbeth. And Iago!"

They both laughed, and Theresa thought she'd never seen such a beautiful smile. She imagined what it would be like to kiss him but quickly felt a rush of embarrassment, since she'd kissed only two boys in her life. Romance was not a familiar topic. Thinking of kissing Kevin conjured up no past experiences of lost love or broken hearts. She'd had no serious relationships. This was fresh territory, and she felt intrigued. Before she could refocus, she heard him say, "Theresa, would you like to get some dinner?"

"Well, sure," she answered, without hesitating.

"Where would you like to go?" Kevin continued, looking a little lost at his own spontaneity.

"Curry," she said. "How about curry?"

"Curry's okay."

Theresa Crandall had opinions. She was rarely hesitant when she had an answer. *Fearless women make conscious choices, when timid men often stumble through options.*

There were warning shots across the bow to let Theresa and Kevin know they were venturing into a whirlwind, but the ship was picking up steam. They dated regularly the remainder of their senior year, talking endlessly, relishing the wonder of a new relationship. She was half fascinated and half in love, and she didn't want to face sorting out the difference. Kevin was shy and smart, and he didn't seem to feel any need to impress her or prove himself. She felt valued and important. She liked his company.

The physical involvement came more slowly. Theresa yearned for him to pull her sweater up over her head and explore her body instead of just hugging with a goodnight kiss. She wore only a silky camisole under her pullovers, and his fingertips had often slid under the edges of the camisole against her lower back. His touch on her warm skin excited her, and she felt hungry sensations beyond their respectful friendship. She imagined being naked with him. Even when he brushed against her or held her hand, she took no initiative in leading him into exploring intimate possibilities, but she ached for him. She was uncertain whether he was avoiding sexual involvement or wanting her to be in charge of it.

As she came out of her last class, and her last exam, Kevin was standing at the foot of the stairs. His exams had finished the day before, and he looked relaxed and especially happy to see her. He wore a fresh, blue cotton shirt with a button-down collar, and the color drew her attention to his deep blue eyes as she came down the stairs toward him. She thought how handsome he was, looking up at her, his eyes taking in her every move.

"For you!" he said, his face flushed with affection and desire. He handed her a bouquet of white roses from behind his back.

"Oh, Kevin, they're beautiful! What's the occasion?" she gasped, trying to hug him without dropping her books and a handful of pens.

"Do I need an occasion?"

"Definitely not! What a wonderful surprise, especially after the exam I just had. It was brutal. Oh, Kevin, can you smell the fragrance?" Theresa momentarily closed her eyes and cradled the tissue-wrapped flowers, oblivious to the smiling students passing by.

"Well," Kevin began again, "there is an occasion. I've been told that white roses are for marriage." He paused, taking a deep breath. "Theresa, I am so in love with you. Will you marry me?"

Theresa opened her eyes wide, blinking. She suddenly became aware of every detail of her surroundings. Students slowed down as they walked by, whispering and staring at the couple talking over white roses. Kevin looked at her with anxious love in his eyes, and all she could think was that her hair was dirty and her clothes looked as though she'd slept in them.

She honestly had no response. She wasn't ready. Kevin looked expectant, hopeful, and she knew she did care deeply for him. *But was it the stuff of marriage?*

A distant clock chimed the half hour. Clouds moved briefly in front of the sun, softening the afternoon light. Theresa wondered how her father had proposed to her mother. Would life with Kevin be what her parents had dreamed for their future? Her eyes followed a low brick wall that meandered in curving turns, as if unable to pursue a straight course.

"It's just too much. Can we talk about this?"

"Of course. I wanted to wait until your exams were over, but I've been so excited, I could barely get through mine! How about pizza in an hour or so?"

"That's perfect. I'll have time to freshen up and feel more like someone worthy of all this." She buried her nose in the white petals, inhaling and feeling the importance of the moment. "I do love you, Kevin. And thank you for these beautiful roses."

Two hours later they huddled over black olive and sausage pizza. Theresa felt so safe with him, as if her heart was sheltered and protected by his. He was an anchor for her rocky ways, and she was the sparkle that brightened his path.

They agreed she would call him one week after going home. They would take time to think, to be certain, far from the college campus that brought them together. *Could their love navigate the unseen waves of success and disappointment, the unknown challenges of the future?*

That night Kevin walked Theresa back to her senior dorm for the last time. The halls were quiet, and her roommate had already left. Boxes and open suitcases were strewn about her room, clothes folded in tidy piles. A brilliant full moon was perfectly framed by the window above her desk. The room was dark and shadowy, with spring breezes carrying the scent of mock orange and the muffled noise of cars.

They sat on her narrow bed, not noticing scattered clothes and the fixed stare of her childhood teddy bear. Kevin gazed sideways out the open window. Their thoughts drifted in the softness of the evening. "A blue moon," he said gently. He slipped his arm around her, kissing her cheek, and burying his face in her dark curls. She loved being close to him and wanted more.

"What's a blue moon?" asked Theresa, leaning into him.

"Truth or dare?" he teased.

"Truth, counselor! The truth, the whole truth, and nothing but the truth," she answered playfully, struggling to get on her knees next to him. Theresa turned toward the window, her body warm against his, and asked again, "What is a blue moon?"

"It's the rare occurrence of a second full moon in one month," he answered, meeting her mischievous eyes. "The scientific derivation is more complicated, but two in a calendar month is enough to go on. It's very unique and special."

The moon held them silhouetted in the window. Kevin turned her toward him and then back onto the soft folds of the feathery quilt. He carefully unbuttoned and removed her blouse and then lifted the silk camisole over her head. She slid her jeans off, and Kevin's trousers fell to the floor on top of hers. They made love for the first time on a narrow little bed in the moonlight of a college memory.

"I love a blue moon," she whispered in his ear.

Three weeks later they were married.

CHAPTER THREE

Theresa was still sitting on the edge of the bed, holding the folded letter from her father, when Kevin came into the room. "The car's all packed, and Gypsy's found her chew toy. Are you okay? I wish you were not making this long journey alone." He moved toward the two suitcases to pick them up.

"I guess I'm a little nervous, now that I'm really going. These last months have stirred up so much emotion. We never know what lies ahead." She sighed. "I'm scared about what I might learn. I'm scared, Kevin, that you and I are drifting apart and that Whimsy Towers will somehow rescue us from the need to sort things out ourselves."

Kevin paused, holding the bags. "I wish we could face this together. Are you sure you don't want to wait and go when I can get off?"

"No, I'll be fine. Really, I will. But there are so many questions, not just about my inheritance, but about us, and we cannot keep avoiding them. I wonder if we can go on, if there is enough to hold us together. We took time apart to decide if getting married was right. Maybe this time apart will help us decide if staying married is right." Her lawyer husband was silent.

Theresa stood up, slipping the letter into her purse.

Looking around the familiar room, with everything so orderly and in its place, she picked up her pillow and sun hat, and followed Kevin toward the hall. Without realizing it, and having never done it before, she closed the door behind her.

The dog was settled in the back seat, as Theresa hugged Kevin and got behind the wheel, kissing him through the open window. "Thanks for doing all this packing, Kevin. The phone should be hooked up when I get there, and I'll call you as soon as I arrive."

Theresa waved as she pulled out of the driveway. In the rear view mirror, she saw Kevin still standing in the street as she turned the corner at the end of the block. She wondered whether she would miss him or feel released. *Some goodbyes linger after the words are finished, and some do not.*

Highway driving dulls the visual senses, but it does provide opportunity to assess the soul. Theresa headed north on Interstate 95, put the car on cruise control, and began to think about Kevin, her father, and her connection to coastal South Carolina. She was anxious to see how a house could be named Whimsy Towers. *And how did her grandmother end up in Cape Cod?*

The hours flew by, with only occasional rest stops for both dog and driver; Theresa wanted to get there before dark. The air cooled as she reached Rhode Island, and she lowered the windows completely to feel the change in temperature. Gypsy, too, showed renewed interest in the trip, sitting up and lifting her nose to catch the unfamiliar breezes.

Coming into Providence, Theresa saw the first signs for Cape Cod. She thought of her college friend Jennifer, who had transferred to the Rhode Island School of Design in Providence. She wondered whether Jenni was still living here making jewelry or had gone on to New York or San Francisco. "Life sometimes jolts us right out of our own footprints," she mused aloud. Gypsy had no comment.

The scenery changed rapidly as she skirted the city. Traffic thinned, and the road divided often. Large chunks of rock jutted at angles from the rolling landscape, some showing signs of massive cutting to allow the road to pass. She saw people working the soil in tidy garden plots with straight rows and wondered what the fresh furrows would hold. *Spring would not wait for indecision.*

At one turn in a quiet area of fields and pasture, she noticed a small white church surrounded by huge trees. As if guarding nobility, the trees stood in perfectly spaced alignment around the sagging building. Black tar paper flapped across one side, and several windows were boarded up. Piles of bricks and stacks of new lumber covered with plastic blocked the front door. A large wooden sign was propped against a tree, facing the highway; its carefully hand-painted letters in bright green said:

THANK YOU, FATHER

WE ARE GROWING

Theresa wanted to pull off and look at that little church, to feel the hope and gratitude expressed by the sign, but she needed to keep moving. A minute was a mile. She made a mental note of the message and continued on her way due east.

Dusk was beginning to settle as Theresa finally arrived in Chatham, Massachusetts. The narrow main street was uncrowded and lined with small shops. Still-bare tree branches spread out overhead, creating an intricate black web across the darkening sky. Quaint clapboard storefronts displayed bathing suits and cotton tops, fine jewelry, and leather goods. Window boxes showed hints of bulbs reaching for spring.

Farther up the street she saw a shop selling homemade candy and ice cream. Along the wide sidewalk, people strolled hand in hand, some shepherding children licking dripping cones and pointing at the windows. It was a leisurely and gracious scene, almost calm. Even the dogs were well behaved.

Theresa's directions to Whimsy Towers led her through the small downtown. The anticipation of seeing the ocean a few blocks ahead made her heart pound; and when she first glimpsed the broad and surprisingly blue water, her foot automatically hit the brake. A startled Gypsy slid onto the floor behind her, but Theresa didn't notice. There it was, the Atlantic Ocean. Its vast chambers held her mother and would soon absorb the remaining link to her parents: the ashes she had brought.

A lookout with parking spaces faced the ocean, and Theresa pulled in and turned off the car. Behind her a lighthouse cast long beams across the neighboring houses and far out toward the watery horizon. She stared at the waves breaking across the distant sand barrier, slowly making their way to shore. *Why couldn't her mother also have found her way to land?*

As she listened to the relentless repeating of the waves, she began to cry and then sob, barely noticing that the dog was trying to lick her cheek.

Other drivers pulled in briefly for a look at the panoramic view. Some got out and stood in front of their cars, breathing deeply as if they wanted to fill themselves with the misty salt air. But most sat still, just looking, engines quiet. Theresa wondered what thoughts they brought to this place.

There were no pictures of Whimsy Towers in her father's belongings, but Theresa had a picture in her mind from her conversations with the bank trustees. Perhaps her father had destroyed photographs to prevent her from knowing about the house and its legacy of painful memories. Or perhaps he had assumed the happy years would go on forever, with plenty of time to record the moments. She had many photographs of herself as a baby, some at the ocean and some on a broad porch or inside a house, but none showed the outside. And none showed her with her mother or grandmother.

Theresa felt as though an intricate family recipe had been handed down through the generations to her, with some of the ingredients left out. These omissions of the past might have resulted from fear of the future or from the random touch of destiny, but she wanted to bring history up to date, filling in the gaps, restoring the recipe. Her ancestors were getting a visitor! She laughed at her philosophical musings. *Was she expecting too much from the gift of an old house?*

The narrow paved road from the lighthouse ended abruptly with a dip onto a gravel surface. An old wooden sign fastened between two posts read, "Proceed only if invited." Sticking out of the top of the sign was a metal rod with a flat, wooden silhouette of a bird. Although faded from long exposure to the sun, its head and body were painted blue, with a small streak of black. Theresa checked her directions to be sure she was not trespassing.

Weathered houses nestled in mulberry trees and hidden by clumps of pine had dotted the road up to this point. Ahead lay thick woods and gnarled underbrush, as if a green oasis had been dropped onto the landscape or risen like Atlantis from a sea of sand. She could hear the faint churning of the ocean, and the only road leading to it was the gravel path in front of her. She eased the car forward, carefully avoiding potholes and fallen branches.

As the drive turned sharply, the trees began to thin, and Theresa glimpsed the side of a house in the distance. It seemed to have its back to her, as if enticing her to come forward and make acquaintance, teasing her to explore its other faces. The car moved ahead slowly, almost drawn on a prearranged course without help from Theresa. Her eyes were fixed on the strange lines of the house and the wood trim ... which appeared to be painted bright pink!

The siding was the familiar cedar shake that she had seen on many houses since her arrival in Cape Cod. Salty breezes and harsh winters had left a warm and rough gray texture, darkened with age in some areas but soft and welcoming. She parked the car and opened the door to get out. As Theresa stepped onto the ground, Gypsy jumped forward into the driver's seat and was out the door right behind her, running full speed toward a cluster of blackbirds, but barking with only half-hearted seriousness. The birds stopped their persistent pecking and took off, easily avoiding her, and the dog squatted slightly to leave her mark.

"Well, I guess you feel right at home, girl!" Theresa laughed.

Her eyes followed the fluttering to the tall oak tree where the birds had fled. The tips of its branches bounced and swayed with dozens of black, feathery extensions.

"Come on, let's check this place out."

As she turned the corner toward the front of the house, she stopped and caught her breath. The dog kept exploring and sniffing, but Theresa stood still and stared at her grandmother's house in the soft sunset of orange shadows. Like a warm embrace, the evening enveloped her. This house had connections to her life that it could not reveal, and she yearned to understand, to step into the past that was held in this quiet place.

It was a two-story house, with a long porch that ran across the entire front and wrapped around the far side.

Large flower pots sat on the steps leading up to the porch, their dead plants still erect, but crisp and brown, as if painted for a ghoulish trick. The porch was white, a shiny white, but the house trim was definitely pink, cotton candy pink. The windows and doors were outlined with it, and the elaborate carving along the roofline was also pink.

But the most arresting feature, incongruous yet appealing, were two tall towers, one at each end of the house. They rose a full story above the top of the roof and had windows and small balconies facing the water. The tower siding was the same cedar shingle as the rest of the house, but the bottom edges were curved at the corners, and they were painted. The tower on the left was green, and the one on the right was bright red. Even in the fading daylight, the colors looked bold and purposeful.

Theresa turned to face the ocean behind her and walked toward the sound of breaking waves. It was getting dark, but she could see the outline of a boathouse and pier, and geese flew low in staggered V-formation, honking with soothing rhythm.

The water that lay before her looked not at all threatening or fierce, but almost playful. Waves curved gently in rolling patterns, and the brilliance of the half moon was enough to catch the curling tops with flashes of light. Theresa closed her eyes, trying to force her memory to acknowledge the sights and sounds of Whimsy Towers, but the effort was futile; she had been too young.

As she started up the steps to the porch, she stopped, looking up to the door as if expecting someone to be there—or to open it for her. The screen door was not locked. She stepped onto the porch—pausing, anxious—wondering what was to come. Expectation breathes trust into the unknown. Like sitting in a hushed and darkened theater before the curtain rises, those who wait and watch relinquish their own reality. The scene comes into view, but the plot evolves slowly.

Her key fit easily into the old lock on the main door. The top half of the door was a large panel of clear glass, surrounded with stained glass squares of deep red and cobalt blue. A design was etched in the center, but she could not make it out with only the moonlight over her shoulder. Theresa stepped inside and ran her fingers along the wall to find a light switch.

As her eyes strained to discern the size or contents of the room, her hand felt several buttons sticking out from the wall, and she instinctively pushed them, one after the other. Almost simultaneously, the room lit up, and the porch behind her filled with light. She was standing in a kitchen, but the certainty of that assumption took a minute to form. It was not an ordinary kitchen, with appliances set in sensible relation to each other or counters defining workspaces.

It was a huge room, perhaps thirty feet long. In one corner was a large fireplace built of irregular pieces of fieldstone, layered horizontally. Chunks of ceramics, colorful tiles, and small wrought-iron shapes stuck out at odd intervals. Two long sofas covered in bold floral print faced the fireplace, and tufted ottomans seemed pushed around at angles to accommodate stretched-out legs.

Theresa looked slowly around the room. Two additional sofas and large stuffed chairs formed comfortable groupings in different places. Books and magazines were piled up on low wicker tables, and the wooden floors were covered with Oriental carpets of blue and red design. She finally saw a stove and built-in refrigerator —actually two separate refrigerators side by side— which made her feel certain this room was the kitchen.

Numerous windows punctuated three walls, though she couldn't see through the growing darkness what the views might be. And between the windows were paint-ings, lots of paintings—big ones and small ones, some with elaborate frames and some with no frames. Modern paintings with splashes of bright color and detailed landscapes hung next to each other, and occasionally a picture had been painted right onto the plain white wall. Signatures and poems were written all over one wall, and comments about some of the paintings were written under them or on the window trim. Theresa felt she had stumbled into the intimacy of a living diary and for a moment feared a tap on the shoulder and someone asking her to leave.

As she looked up at the two massive chandeliers in the middle of the room, she noticed that the ceiling was painted dark blue, with swirling clouds and star formations. Angels in diaphanous gowns peered down as if watching the activity below. One held out a nautical life preserver ring that said "Too Late." Another held a gorgeous cake with layers of white frosting decorated with yellow flowers and little people on top. Another cradled a baby wrapped snugly in pink blankets. Others were smiling or crying, sometimes holding hands or waving. The work was detailed and exquisite. The trompe l'oeil was done so brilliantly that Theresa thought she could reach up and receive the outstretched baby or run her finger across the cake to taste its flavor. Whimsy Towers was drawing her into its illusions of reality.

Still craning her neck to observe the beautiful angels, she leaned against one of the two refrigerator doors and held onto the handle to balance herself. Slowly lowering her gaze, and wondering whether anything might still be inside, she pulled the door open. She gasped, letting out a startled sound. The open door did not reveal a refrigerator at all, but a solid wall decorated with photographs and crayon scribbles on colored paper. She quickly opened the other door and felt oddly relieved to see the bare metal shelves of a real refrigerator.

What had appeared to be two identical refrigerators was also a visual trick, and Theresa marveled at how convincing it was. *A refrigerator door securely hinged to a wall!* She opened the first door again and suddenly realized she was literally looking into her past, into her grandmother's heart, into a vault of memories. She had opened the door to the history she craved. Directly in front of her was a photograph of a laughing, smiling woman about her age, holding a dark-haired baby up close to her face. The woman looked exactly like Theresa.

Her knees weakened, but her body stayed still, held in place by her eyes' fixed stare. Both woman and baby were wearing bathing suits, and they sat on the steps to Whimsy Towers, next to the large pots then filled with blossoming bushes and life. The baby's legs were covered with sand, as if she'd been dipped in honey and rolled in fine oats. Mother and child. Emily and Theresa. Other snapshots tacked to the wall showed Theresa sleeping or playing in her mother's lap and reading books on the porch swing with both her parents. Her father was young and happy and clearly in love.

Theresa's father would tell her about those days with a faraway look in his eyes that troubled her and kept his emotions at a distance. Loneliness crept in like a silent companion, reminding him of loss and filling him with emptiness. She knew he had been given only a limited time with the woman he loved, and the promise of it all had been taken from him.

Theresa's parents had met in college on a blind date and had married secretly just before graduation. Summer after college can be a time of blind optimism, time to exhale, to revel in accomplishments and dream new dreams, and the newlyweds moved into Whimsy Towers with Emily's mother. Love kept all the world at bay, and discouragement did not knock, admitting the reality of limited options. An easy routine developed, with long days spent walking the beach, berry picking, biking sand trails, and reading books of no consequence. Emily was an expert sailor.

By the end of that first September, as the days cooled and shook loose the carefree summer, Emily realized she was pregnant. It was a well-received surprise, and Theresa was born on a blustery, cold morning of early Cape spring—April first. Her grandmother Theodosia emptied the small local shops of every item necessary for a new baby. Her mother wanted to call her April, but her father told her he'd insisted he would not make it so easy for anyone to call his child "April Fool."

Weeks rolled into months, with Theresa's first steps in a grown-up world. Her father worked for an advertising agency in the next town, and her mother and grandmother painted frolicking nursery rhyme characters all over the walls and ceiling of Theresa's room. Her father had smiled at the recollection of how he'd come home from work in an office to these artist women in his life. No one could know that they would soon be separated.

It was an accident. A boating accident was all Theresa's father had ever said about her mother's death, before his final letter was discovered in the metal box. He could not even say the words without tears filling his eyes, and she could not bear to cause him the pain of remembering. He had packed up his little daughter, not yet two years old, and moved to northern Virginia; but a new life could not cover the mystery of the past forever. Theresa had come to Whimsy Towers for answers, and she was beginning to blame her father for the years of silence and denial. He did not have the right to hide the past. *Omissions are lies dressed up to deflect the truth.*

These photographs showed that her mother was built much like Theresa—slim and agile, with dark hair that was longer and less curly. Theresa's curls had come from her father, but the color was definitely her mother's dusty coal. And their noses had the same straight angle, with just a hint of lift at the end.

On the inside of the door that formed the cover of this refrigerator family album, Theresa saw boxes of crayons and little stuffed animals lined up on the shelf racks. As she reached for a small teddy bear, she heard muffled whining from the porch and realized she had left the dog outside. She automatically closed the refrigerator door as if to trap the cold air inside after she'd retrieved a gallon of milk. The latch caught with a thump, leaving the photo images imprinted on memory and sealed again from view.

"Oh, Gypsy, I'm sorry, girl. Do you wonder what's going on here? Come on in."

The dog went straight into the kitchen and began to sniff the carpets as if expecting to find recent crumbs or spills. Her tail wagged in rhythm with her step, and she sniffed the floor in purposeful pursuit. She stopped occasionally for a tentative lick or to sneeze a low-lying cobweb off her nose.

Theresa laughed. "The cupboard is bare, Gypsy. There hasn't been a good crumb available here in a long while.

Let's see the rest of the place, and then I'll bring in our food from the car."

She stepped into the dark adjacent room, with her dog close at her heels.

Theresa's hand found the push buttons for the light as easily as if she'd done it a thousand times. The room was sparsely furnished. In the center was a long table with a white top; ten or twelve chairs lined the sides. A wooden highchair with a child's silver cup on the tray sat against the wall. Above it was a large portrait in a heavily gilded frame. Theresa felt pulled towards the picture as if drawn by a magnet.

People and events were coming together too quickly. Lack of introduction and instant familiarity blended like swirls of custard. Her heart knew these faces, but her memory gave no sound to their voices or feel of their touch. The portrait depicted a woman relaxing comfortably in an oversized, upholstered chair, surrounded by blue and white striped pillows. On the arm of the chair perched a smiling young girl of ten or twelve, leaning against the woman. Her small hand was cradled in the woman's hands, resting in her lap. They looked utterly content and happy.

Theresa clicked on a small light hanging over the picture and bent forward to look at it more closely. "Hello, Grandmother," she said aloud. She stared at the figure of the seated woman, whose chestnut hair and large, mischievous eyes looked not at all like her daughter's. Emily's hair was dark and straight. She wore a fuzzy blue sweater with matching skirt, and her leg dangled easily over the arm of the chair as if she often sat that way with her mother.

Behind the two figures in the portrait was an open window with curtains flapping in the breeze and a distant sailboat on a broad expanse of calm, blue water. Theresa tried to read the name of the boat, but the letters were too small; it appeared to be two words. The entire scene was one of peace and sunlight. She fantasized putting herself into the portrait, clasping hands with her mother and grandmother, sharing the sense of acceptance and completeness she saw in their eyes. *Could she spread her wings without knowing more of her roots?* She stared into the eyes of the portrait and wondered for the first time whether she had made the right decision to come here. Whimsy Towers was their story; she and Gypsy were disturbing the dust.

The dining room table caught her attention as she ran her hand across the cool surface. The top was a huge piece of white marble, not smooth like a tombstone, but slightly rough, like the feel of an orange. Subtle shades of gray whirled in random patterns. Chiseled in large, rounded letters along one side were the words "TABLE OF THE MUSES." The top rested on six wooden bases, carved like sections of a totem pole. Faces and birds and nonsense figures peered out in all directions. It was an extraordinary table, and Theresa wondered how many men would have been required to carry such a slab of marble. *Did it come from Italy? Did Emily's real father send it? And who were the muses?*

New revelations were creating new questions for Theresa, and she was beginning to feel tired from the long day. Suddenly, she remembered she had promised to call Kevin. She glanced at her watch and realized he would be getting worried. She was not good at keeping track of time. Her days of free-lance writing and illustrating were open spaces for creative work, not chopped into time segments dictated by habit. Kevin had given her the watch, probably in hopes that she would notice how a day was outlined or that mealtimes had a certain regularity. She rarely wore it.

Stepping back into the kitchen, she spotted a telephone on a round table in front of a window. Gypsy followed her and lay contentedly at her feet, stretched out across a pattern of ivory-colored doves in the carpet.

"Oh, Kevin, you wouldn't believe this place! It's so beautiful, and I'm a little overwhelmed already."

"What kind of overwhelmed? What's the house like? Any surprises?"

"It's tucked away, off the road. Very private. And Kevin ..." She paused, feeling tears starting to form as she blinked. "I've seen pictures of my mother. I look a lot like her."

"Are you okay?"

"Yes, but it's been quite a day. The house appears to be in good condition, but I've only seen the first couple of rooms. It's half home and half art gallery! Gypsy seems very relaxed. She made a run for some birds but is sleeping on the only ones she'll likely get near; they're woven in the carpet!"

"I'm glad the phone works. Did you get some food? Do you have what you need?" Kevin was good with loose ends and details. It was the big picture that often eluded him, but Theresa could hear his concern.

"I passed some little shops on my way through town, but I imagine the bigger stores are farther out. Tomorrow I'll explore. It's a really beautiful area, and the ocean is so close to the house."

She struggled to lift the window sash. "I bet you can hear the ocean yourself. Hold on." The window slid up; Theresa felt cool, moist air and heard the sound of waves lapping on the shore or against pilings or rocks near the boathouse. Holding the phone against the screen, she called in the background, "Hear it?"

But Kevin could not hear the water. "I'll have to take your word for it. Tell me about the house? Do you like it? Any ghosts?"

"Ghosts?" She laughed. "I think I'm the ghost! I'm the one out of place here, stepping into someone else's life, looking at their things—like an intruder moving tentatively through a stranger's house."

"Do you feel comfortable staying there alone?" he asked.

"Oh, yes. Though I haven't seen the whole house yet, I have my ferocious watchdog." She looked down at her sleeping companion. Gypsy's gray hairs were only slightly noticeable in the fur around her mouth and on her paws. She was still a shiny golden color, with shades of blonde disguising the gray. They had bought her as soon as Kevin got out of law school, and they doted on her like the parents of an only child. Gentle and sweet-natured, Gypsy showed no preference between them.

Kevin laughed. "Oh, right! I know that mean dog. She'd certainly scare anybody away with her snoring! Do you have any neighbors?"

"Not that I can see from the house. Whimsy Towers is really protected behind trees and runaway bushes. Some kind of wild rose, I think. But these two amazing towers stick up above the roofline, and I bet there's quite a view. I'll let you know in the daylight."

"Well, I'm glad you arrived safely, Theresa. I've been thinking about you and thinking about our marriage. We're playing for high stakes here, and I do want to make us work. Call me tomorrow?"

"I will."

"Goodnight."

"Goodnight" repeated like an echo in Theresa's head. She was not used to being away from Kevin. They didn't have much practice in farewells or reassuring expressions of devotion. Their life together rumbled along with familiar routine and steadiness—no flurries of emotion, no passionate reunions after time apart. They didn't know about separation. She was on her own for the first time, stirring up the deep waters of familiarity. Neither Kevin nor her father could hold her hand—or keep her back.

As Theresa put down the phone, she breathed in

deeply the moist ocean air, closing her eyes to shut out any distraction from the sweetness of wild roses. She felt strangely content. For a few minutes she lingered at the open window, eyes closed, her thoughts reaching forward and backward as she tried to knot them in the center—the present moment. She felt at home.

Ducks made low, squawking sounds as they settled into the marsh, and the cool night air tingled her upturned face, trying to break the spell of blind reverie. The breeze began to take on the faint sound of distant music, like heaven's guitars hidden in the blackened clouds. At first lulled by dreamy comfort, she accepted the eerie, almost melancholy sound. But when she opened her eyes, the music continued. She looked out the window and saw a light in the direction of the boathouse. Perhaps someone is out for a moonlight cruise, she thought. Someone alone with his thoughts and the music that comforts him. It did not occur to her that perhaps it was lovers alone with music that arouses them.

CHAPTER FOUR

Theresa closed the window and walked back toward the dining room, not stopping to notice paintings or portraits or shelves loaded with trinkets. She wanted to see the rest of the house. There would be time, plenty of time, to retrace her steps; this house was hers now. As she passed the dining room table, she undid her watch and laid it on the cold, hard surface.

The next room was a surprise. Expecting to see a living room, she found long wooden tables with jars and tubes of paint and paintbrushes of various lengths in careful rows. Half a dozen easels stood throughout the room, several holding unfinished paintings and the others empty, like stiff and silent caretakers. In one corner was a low easel. Theresa walked slowly towards it. In childish lettering, with each letter a different bright color, the name *Claude* was spelled across the top.

Who was Claude? She had never heard her father say the name. She ran her fingers across the letters, as if hoping their mystery could be revealed through touch. The other easels had no names. They were turned in ways that would allow the artist to see out a window or toward a platform where a model might have posed.

Against one wall was the oversized chair she had seen in the dining room portrait. The blue and white pillows looked faded and limp, but Theresa sank into the chair and pulled them around her, feeling their softness. The dusty smell of old upholstered furniture and the clutter of paints and paintings around the room soothed her and let her thoughts slip off to sleep.

It was Gypsy that startled her back from dozing, and Theresa awoke with the momentary confusion of being in a strange place. She had been dreaming of Kevin. They were driving on an ice-layered road in Virginia. Trees bent and dipped with the impossible weight of snow, branches snapping and falling in the path of the car. She repeatedly called out to him to be careful, but he drove silently on, calmly avoiding every obstacle and remaining oblivious to the deafening crash of trees around him. As she frantically reached over to grab his arm, she realized he was wearing only a bathing suit! Tightening her grip, she felt the hairs on his arm between her fingers as she yelled, "Kevin, stop the car! Stop!"

Gypsy jumped and yelped as she pulled away from the chair, and Theresa's hand fell from gripping the dog's back. Tufts of blonde fur stuck between her fingers, and Gypsy's coat was ruffled and pulled in odd directions toward her tail, as if a bird had foraged around to stir up the makings of a nest. The old dog moved several feet from the chair to lie down again, keeping her eyes fixed on Theresa.

The room was dark, chilly, and not yet separate from

the dream of being with Kevin. Theresa's body, still curled awkwardly in the large chair, felt stiff and tense. She blinked and stretched; pillows fell to the floor. The nap had slowed her tour of the house, and she pulled her reluctant thoughts from her icy dream to the present. The room seemed smaller than just an hour before. The easels cast long purple shadows on the floor, and curtains hung like ghosts at the windows. She remembered them from the portrait of her mother and grandmother. No longer billowy and fresh, they too had lost life.

She stood and walked to each window, carefully removing the once-white curtains. Gypsy didn't follow her or even move until Theresa said aloud, "Guess we're beginning to redecorate." Her voice seemed to signal a return to normalcy for the dog. With brisk step, Theresa carried an armload of yesterday's curtains to the kitchen, and her tousled companion followed with jaunty little steps of anticipation.

"Hungry?" she asked over her shoulder. "Let's bring in some food; I'm starved."

A slow-moving caravan of dark clouds had blotted out the earlier evening stars, and the moon lacked sufficient brilliance to pierce them. Theresa looked toward the ocean. She again saw a light in the direction of the boathouse. She couldn't make out the surroundings in the dark and wondered whether the light had moved or whether her sense of direction was skewed. She listened for music but heard only the unfamiliar night sounds of owls and a loon.

The sky spread out above her like a frayed and porous canopy, arching over Whimsy Towers with a protective curl. Theresa watched the drifting somber clouds and shuddered. Part of her wished that Kevin were here to share this adventure, and part of her wanted to keep it safe and separate and sheltered from the life she had with him. *He never saw faces in clouds or stopped to breathe in the air of new places. For him a house was a house, not a touchstone of the soul.*

It took only a few minutes to unload the groceries. Gypsy bounded across the expanse of lawn, darting from the car to shadowy bushes and back again. Occasionally she did a run and roll, lingering with her legs in the air and squirming to scratch her back. With each trip to the house, Theresa called, "I'll be right back," as if reassuring a child in strange surroundings. But Gypsy showed no fear of the unknown. Exploration was her game, and her fenced yard in Virginia had just lost its boundaries.

Theresa carried her suitcases and blankets into the house and whistled for Gypsy. With her familiar things strewn around the kitchen carpet and on the couches and tables, the blending of past and present had begun. The visitors were here to stay. At least for awhile. She opened her cooler and pulled out a ham and cheese sandwich, with mustard-covered tomato and sprouts oozing from the side.

"Not exactly tidy travel food!" She laughed, poking the runaway sprouts back between the bread. She handed Gypsy a large dog biscuit and settled down with her sandwich and an apple in front of the silent fireplace. She imagined a crackling fire, with marshmallows and chestnuts roasting. Her eyes focused on the bits of pottery and ceramic cemented in with the fieldstone. Colorful tiles had drawings of stick figures and simple flowers under glowing suns. Theresa stood up to read the letters in the corner of one tile. They spelled out *Claude* in irregular sizes and uneven spacing. The picture on the tile was a solitary boat; above it was a black cloud.

"Ready for the next level?" Theresa called to Gypsy, leaving the last bites of sandwich on a pile of magazines. "Let's see what the sleeping arrangements are."

The wide staircase turned sharply half way to the second floor, allowing the climber to suddenly see a broad open hall straight ahead. Each step brought more of the space into view. With only the backlight from the stairwell, she could see massive lattice arches and the tops of statuary. When she reached the floor, she saw a switch; and with a click, soft light filled the room from no discernable source. Above the door was a beautifully hand-painted sign that said "OUTDOORS INDOORS."

Statues and garden furniture were placed around the room. Large urns filled with dirt stood prominently in the center, surrounding a dry fountain with plump cherubs holding water buckets. Small empty planters and pots of various shapes were scattered in clusters, but there was not a sign of a plant, even a dead one. At one window was a pedestal birdbath, and Theresa noticed that the window sill was scratched and pecked. Child-sized chairs mingled with elegant iron benches and a massive sundial that had the greenish look of submerged bronze.

In the center of the ceiling was a large skylight, covering most of the area of the room. Dozens of crystal stars on invisible string hung around the edges, catching the light and throwing it back. The room was a garden party waiting to happen. With a bold brush of lush greenery and a tray of lemonade, Theresa could imagine laughing and relaxing in the warmth of this sunny hideaway. *Outdoors indoors. Perhaps Grandmother had discovered the answer to long Cape Cod winters.*

From the deserted garden, several doors led to other rooms. The first one appeared to be the master bedroom. It was large, yellow, and chock-full of beautifully carved antique furniture. Walnut or cherry, wondered Theresa, as she rubbed her hand along the curved edges. She was not surprised to see paintings on all the walls. She was beginning to realize that paintings were more than decoration at Whimsy Towers; they were the heart of the place—and the bones.

Two other bedrooms were comfortably furnished, and Theresa was thinking about where she might like to sleep as she stepped into a small adjoining room. Her mouth fell open and her eyes widened. She could not move forward. Nursery rhyme characters and pudgy animals danced over the walls in colors still brilliant after thirty-four years. Flowers were painted on vines that climbed to the ceiling. Clowns held balloons and cupcakes. This was the first room of her childhood, the nursery that welcomed her home as a new baby, the room created by her mother and grandmother that her father had described—the room left behind when life began anew in Virginia.

A white crib and white furniture painted with rag dolls still stood ready. Theresa wondered why the room remained intact. The furniture looked a little nicked and tired, and she smiled to think that she must have been rough as a youngster, but she had no memory of it. She felt love in the room—the love given to a baby and the love of gratitude for the giving.

Theresa walked back to the master bedroom, stretched out on the large bed, and cried herself to sleep. She spent her first night at Whimsy Towers fully dressed, on her grandmother's Double Wedding Ring quilt, her dog sleeping peacefully at the door. All the lights in the house were still on, lighting up the shadows of the past.

Theresa awoke to the sound of birds, not faint chirping, but bold, jungle sounds. Bright light filled the room as a new day caught the sun rising slowly from the ocean. She lay still, remembering her first impressions of Whimsy Towers. She wondered how many times she must have sat or played on this bed with her grandmother or parents. She felt the bumpy hand-stitching of the large, interlocking wedding rings on the quilt beneath her. Its colorful fabric was pieced together with delicate precision and order—each piece belonging to the overall pattern, each piece fitting perfectly into the balance of the design.

The windows in the room were tall and had no curtains. Grandmother must not have felt the need for privacy or sleeping late in a darkened room. Birds signaled the call to rise; the day began with nature's clock. The tops of oak trees brushed against the window panes, with small branches squeaking across the surface. Theresa watched the gentle motion of new leaves. The rhythm of the swaying branches stirred memories of her childhood tree house in Virginia.

"Be careful up there," her father had called when he saw her leaning too far off the unfinished platform. "Stay back from the edge until I have the walls up."

She liked standing at the edge, feeling close to the tree's enormous limbs and looking down with the same view as the birds. No walls separated her from the sensation of living in the branches, and she dared herself to look down without holding on.

Theresa knew she had been too reckless as a child. She had wanted the tree house to be higher in the old oak. She loved to climb its gnarled branches and hide in the thick clusters of leaves, above the safety of the tree house. When strong northern winds blew, she crawled toward the narrowing end of the branches and held on with the fearless determination of a bronco rider. The wind whipped through her hair until it almost stood on end, and she gripped the coarse bark so tightly it left marks on her fingers.

Still swaying in her thought, Theresa absently

watched a gaggle of blackbirds fly out of sight from the
tree at the window. Unconsciously, she'd wrapped her
fingers tightly around the soft folds of the quilt, pulling it
up snugly on both sides of her. Her hands ached from the
strain. She relaxed her grip and thought how the blackbirds might return to their tree, but others who had sung
their songs here were gone, with no return. Rising from
her grandmother's bed, Theresa instinctively smoothed
the covers and then stretched out her fingers, rubbing
her hands together to loosen the tension.

"Breakfast?" she called to Gypsy, who was standing
ready at the door.

They emerged from the bedroom into the garden
room, and Theresa stopped to notice how light filtered
down through the skylight, resting on statues and casting
gentle shadows through the lattice. Plants would love
this space, she thought; and she wondered how foolish it
would be to buy plants for just the short time she would
be staying.

Gypsy hurried down the stairs ahead, and Theresa followed her without stopping as she retraced her steps
from the night before. When they got to the kitchen,
Theresa turned off the lights and headed for the porch.
As she opened the door to go outside, she bumped something that fell off to the side. She looked down and saw a
corncob, partly chewed at one end. Kernels of corn and
circles of cut carrots were scattered on the steps and in
the dirt.

As Gypsy sniffed eagerly around the scene, Theresa

picked up the moist corncob. "Looks like someone wants to share dinner with us. Or breakfast."

She could understand how a stray corncob might end up at her door with a squirrel or raccoon, but the precisely cut carrot pieces were troubling. Theresa looked around her, as if the answer would become suddenly apparent. Instead, what greeted her was the incredible beauty of nature's wonder and welcome.

A carefully mowed green carpet of lawn stretched toward the water. Only a few small trees stood on this side of the house, providing an unobstructed, broad view. A slight inlet or cove served as a buffer for the land from the ocean, and the strip of ground that protected the inlet was fortified with huge rocks in irregular clumps. As she walked across the grass, Theresa saw wooden steps leading to the boathouse she had glimpsed at dusk. It sat on sturdy pilings and had a small window facing the main house.

Far behind the weathered building were lingering bits of orange and pink clouds, laced with yellow, that hung on the morning horizon. She watched the changing colors as she found her way to the door on the side and opened it cautiously. Inside was one large room. Several life preservers were piled in the corner, and a collection of oars and paddles leaned against the rough wooden wall. There was no other evidence of boats or boating.

A bed with rumpled sheets and blankets looked as though it had been recently used. Next to the bed was a low table with a large portable radio and tape player.

Cassette tapes were lined up in careful piles, each facing the same direction in order to display the titles. Except for the bed, the room looked orderly and clean.

A large round oak table with four straight chairs stood in the middle. On it were old sports magazines and books of poetry by Carl Sandburg and Robert Frost. An apple, two carrots, and a knife lay on a plate. Theresa froze. *Carrots.* She turned to face the door and heard quickening steps on the wooden planks outside. Before she could react or decide where to hide, Gypsy appeared in the open doorway, wagging her tail.

"Oh, Gypsy!" she gasped. "You scared me half to death!"

As she turned to leave, Theresa passed a large, stuffed chair that faced a window looking out on the water. Next to it was an upside-down crate used as an end table, with several unopened cans of soda and bags of chips. She stooped down to read the expiration date on the bags. It was then she realized she was not alone at Whimsy Towers.

CHAPTER FIVE

Hello? Yes, I'll wait," Theresa said, trying to sound calm and businesslike. Her heart still pounded, partly from the fright in the boathouse and partly from running all the way back across the lawn to the phone. Gypsy could hardly keep up with her.

She had spoken to the bank trustees many times since her father's death and the revelation that she had inherited her grandmother's property. They had settled the real estate by mail and agreed that she would come into the bank to receive things from the safe deposit box. Grandmother had left some jewelry and letters, nothing that couldn't wait for Theresa's arrival in Chatham. But her question could not wait for a trip to the bank.

"Hello?"

"Hello. This is Theresa Crandall."

"Well, hello. Are you in town? Is everything in good order at the house? I hope you found it all right."

"Yes, yes. The house is fine, but … " She hesitated, wondering how to ask. "Is someone else living here?"

"Someone else? What do you mean? The house has been empty since your grandmother died."

"I believe someone has been using the boathouse. I found food and things there this morning."

"Food? We have not given anyone permission to be at your grandmother's house. After she died, her nurse needed time to relocate, but they moved over a year ago."

"They?"

"Yes, she had a son. Because of her long service and devotion to your grandmother, we allowed her to stay in the house to keep things going while we held the house in trust for you. She is still in the area but has her own place."

"Would the caretaker be staying there?" asked Theresa, anxious to make sense of her mystery visitor and to quiet her fear.

"Rick? Not likely. He lives in town and teaches at the community college. Lost his wife a few years back and looks after properties to fill in the extra time. Nice man. We were really sorry about his wife, but I don't think he'd have any reason to hang around your place. He cut the grass last week, but I collected the keys from him since he won't need to be checking inside for us anymore. You might like to connect with him about yard work or projects around the house. He's a good worker."

"Thanks, I will." Theresa paused, debating whether to ask this man she'd never met a question that might reveal more than she was ready for. "Just one last question."

"Yes?"

"Do you know anything about the two towers at the house or why they are painted red and green?"

"I wish I did. I've often wondered about that myself." He laughed. "Your grandmother set up her will and accounts here many years before I came. I understand she was quite a character, decisive and headstrong, but always interested in others. By the time I met her, the bank was already handling her affairs, and she was pretty confused mentally. But she always smiled and warmly shook my hand, as if I were the most important visitor in the world. The last time I saw her, on a gorgeous, sunny afternoon, she took my arm and whispered, 'Don't go sailing today. It's dangerous.' I assured her I would not; the water makes me seasick."

Theresa tried to imagine the beautiful woman with chestnut hair that she saw in the dining room portrait as an aged, frail dowager, out of touch with reality and drifting on a current of lost memory and longing. It saddened her to think her grandmother had no family in her last years. She wondered whether she could have made a difference. *And how could her father, the most loving man she knew, turn his back on his mother-in-law during the years when her heart and mind were sinking?*

"Thank you," Theresa stuttered, her voice cracking. "I do appreciate all your help and your taking such good care of the house. I love being here, and I'll stop in the bank soon to get the safe deposit things. And Rick's phone number."

"That'll be fine. We'll keep in touch. And if there's anything funny going on there, call the police. This is a quiet sort of town, but no point taking chances. One other thing, Theresa, just to keep in mind. We have a standing offer to buy Whimsy Towers, if you decide you don't want to hold onto it. Your grandmother had a good eye, and it's a valuable piece of property. These buyers have deep pockets, and they're patient. I told them I'd let you know."

Theresa hung up and sighed deeply. She was being asked to consider possibilities for the future before she even knew where she fit in the present. Looking around the kitchen, she gathered up items she had brought from the car and put them in the cupboards. She liked the feel of the old cupboard doors, smooth and softened, their painted edges worn to bare wood by the rubbing fingers of the past. She put several bottles of juice and cartons of creamy fruit yogurt from the cooler into the refrigerator. And as she closed the door, her other hand pulled open the adjacent one that revealed the photographs from the night before.

She stared at the faces, trying hard to remember. *Such smiles and happiness!* The faded black and white memories were not her memories. Theresa could compare only her father as she remembered him with these pictures of a young man so at ease with his family, so comfortable and happy. The pictures of her mother and grandmother were fixed in time, with no attachment to another time or place for her. They were history's record. These women from her life had played another stage, and there was no encore.

Theresa was particularly drawn to one photograph of her father carrying her on his shoulders along the sandy beach. They were walking toward the cameraperson, her father laughing and Theresa anxiously holding out shells or stones, as if the camera could take them or the photographer was to put the camera down and take the shells or the child. She easily remembered the feeling of riding on her father's shoulders, but it was through crowds at parades and not along beaches strewn with sea treasures.

He was a quiet man. His life was the raising of his daughter. Theresa realized as never before how difficult it must have been for him to see her go off to college and then to marriage, to let go of another woman that he loved.

She wanted to call Kevin. She wanted to talk about their relationship. She wanted to see hope in their future, but she remembered the pain of their last evening together before she left. They had been in the den, listening to a tape of a piano concerto they both enjoyed. He was working at his desk, and she was sketching aimlessly.

The ice in Theresa's lemonade had almost melted, diluting the flavor and leaving small bits of ice struggling between soggy mint leaves. She sighed as she took a sip. She could not tell Kevin that her tasteless, watery lemonade was a metaphor for their marriage. She could not tell Kevin much of anything. She wrestled with feelings of suffocation and the desire for emotional intimacy, the need to be herself and still be loved. A bird gives up its freedom of flight to be an object of beauty and wonder, but not willingly. It does not choose to be caged.

"What's on your mind?" he inquired, without looking

up from his work. "You seem lost in thought."

She hesitated, not sure where, or whether, to begin.

Kevin was balancing the checkbook. "Theresa, don't you think you could enter the check amounts in the white lines instead of the gray? It throws me off when you skip a space."

He was serious. Theresa resisted the temptation to get up and leave the room. Avoidance was easier than confrontation, but she would be leaving for several weeks and didn't want to spend the last evening fuming alone over friction in their marriage.

"What in the world difference does it make?" she asked, putting down her drink with a thump. It splashed onto the table. "There are pages and pages of lines, Kevin; they're not each allotted to a specific function or check. It really doesn't matter which color line is used."

Kevin looked up and responded, as if to a bank customer, "But the white lines are for the check amounts and deposits. The gray lines reflect the balance." He did not know how to get into the emotion of an issue.

Theresa felt tears welling up. "Finding fault with me over silly things is not healthy for us. I feel like I'm on a roller coaster of approval and disapproval. I cannot always follow instructions that seem obvious to you. The checks and deposits are there, in order."

"I think you're over-reacting."

Theresa took a deep breath and pulled her leg out from under her, causing one of the cushions to fall to the floor. *Little irritations build up mountains of hurt.* A long, slow series of ten clock chimes urged a cease-fire.

"I don't think this is really about the lines in the checkbook, Kevin. It's about flexibility and tolerance. It's about partnership. I just feel as though I'm heading for a trap at every turn, an opportunity for inadequacy." She hesitated. "I think you need someone who does not question you and always paints between the lines."

Theresa went off to bed alone, feeling empty and confused.

Ↄ

Gypsy was waiting patiently to see where her breakfast would be served. She sat watching Theresa during the phoning and the reverie, but once-a-day eating had its urgency. She rubbed her nose against Theresa's leg.

"Okay, I get the message, girl. Let's eat." She filled the dog's water bowl and then scooped up a mixture of dry food and dumped it into a yellow plastic bowl. "Bon appetit," she said as she stroked the dog's back. Bits of winter fur were already starting to come loose, a sure harbinger of warm weather.

Grabbing a blueberry bagel from a bag, Theresa slipped off to explore the remaining part of the house: the towers. Sunlight streamed through the windows of each room as she headed back upstairs. The paintings she'd seen the night before had new life and intensity. The furniture felt familiar. Every room had views of the ocean, and she stopped often to open windows, looking each time for signs of activity at the boathouse.

When she got to the garden landing, there were no doors leading up to the towers, so she returned to her grandmother's yellow room. Opening each door that seemed like a closet, she found one that revealed dark-stained stairs that wound upward at sharp angles. Slowly, Theresa climbed the shadowy stairwell. It felt like a vertical tunnel, with light filtering down from above.

"Hello?" she called, and then felt foolish as she heard nothing but her own voice. The unseen was the unknown, but there was no reasonable expectation of meeting anyone in the tower. She wondered for a moment whether this was the red or the green one. The expression "bats in the belfry" darted across her mind, and she looked up as she climbed. A sturdy handrail followed along with the turn of the steps, and Theresa was grateful for a firm grip as she strained her eyes to see what lay ahead.

The steps ended at a platform-like space. In the middle was a huge fixed light, similar to a lighthouse lens. It was cradled in a short chimney structure that had panels of red glass separated by white sectors. On one wall, wide French doors opened towards the ocean. Windows of solid-paned clear glass were on the other three walls.

"My grandmother, the lighthouse keeper!" Theresa laughed aloud.

She opened the doors and gingerly tested the small balcony with her foot to see whether it felt secure enough to hold her. She was no longer fond of heights, and insecurity combined with height was an unpleasant prospect. A momentary sensation of looking down from her childhood tree house flashed through her mind. During that period of fearlessness in her life, there had been someone there to warn her of danger.

She remained grounded in the doorway, but the view was spectacular. The ocean used up all her eyes. It drew her in so completely that she didn't notice she was holding her breath, until she gasped for lack of air.

Small fishing boats were silhouetted against the silver sparkle of the water, each rocking gently with the current. The bows lifted and then dipped as the waves rolled under and then hurried on.

Theresa could see individual fishermen in some of the boats, and she wondered who they were and where they lived and what they were catching. She imagined fathers teaching sons to fish, and each generation telling tales of the sea to the anxious ears of those who followed. She wondered whether her grandmother had developed such an intimate connection to the ocean—and whether she blamed it for the drowning of her only child.

The day was clear, and the rising sun cleaned the sky as it moved higher on the horizon. Theresa closed her eyes and thought of Grandmother Theodosia standing on this balcony, watching her family play on the sandy beach or later staring at the water and yearning for her lost daughter. Whimsy Towers had weathered the sunshine and storms of the northeast coast and the personal seasons of its occupants. The house remained; the seasons would repeat.

Theresa was anxious to find the other tower, so she climbed down the stairs and checked the bedrooms until she found another door leading up. Similar steps led her to a second platform with a huge light. This one was cloaked in green glass, and similar doors and windows as the other tower surrounded it. She assumed the light's color corresponded to the paint color of the tower, but she could not be sure without venturing out onto the balconies to see the house. Red and green towers; red and green lights. *What was the reason? And did Grandmother create this curiosity?*

Theresa spent the remainder of the morning bringing things in from the car and putting them away. She hung the two hanging baskets of pink petunias on the porch and stepped back to admire them. "Just right." She smiled.

She liked the feel of the porch and was surprised that the furniture cushions had a floral pattern similar to one she had selected for her own screened porch. She and Grandmother liked pink flowers, but the bright pink trim on the house was still beyond Theresa's grasp. Life choices can, and sometimes should, defy the logical, she thought. And remembering the bank trustee saying her grandmother was "a character," she said aloud, "Good for you, Theodosia Hampton; you had guts."

Now that the Jeep was empty and the dog snored contentedly next to her birds, Theresa was ready to explore the town. She wondered whether people locked their doors here and decided against the idea. Leaving Gypsy in charge of security, she drove the car back down the bumpy gravel drive. "Red Rover," she said, tapping her hand twice on the dashboard. "You shall be called 'Red Rover.' You've brought me on quite an adventure." Another affectionate tap, and the matter was sealed.

More people were on the streets midday than Theresa had seen the evening before on her way through town. There was not the sense of a beach town or casual resort area. Women were smartly dressed, with matching blouses and pressed slacks. They wore cardigan sweaters with bold brassy buttons and small embroidered designs. Many walked purposefully, carrying bags from shops and greeting others on the sidewalk. Theresa noticed handbags of delicately woven basketry, with carved scrimshaw on top, and wrists loaded with gold bracelets. These women did not have sand between their toes.

It was easy to park the car, and Theresa left Red Rover in front of the ice cream shop and walked down Main Street to the bank. The trust officers were at lunch, but a package was waiting for her, and the receptionist asked whether she'd like to open it in a private room. "No, thank you," she replied, lifting the box to test the weight. "I'll just take it along."

She signed for the package and saw a phone number taped to the top. It said "Rick's phone. Don't lose." How nice to be so valuable, she thought.

A two-scoop strawberry ice cream cone sounded like just the right lunch, and Theresa carried her grandmother's safe deposit secrets into the shop that boasted "the best homemade fudge and ice cream." Being somewhat of an expert on this topic, she sat at a round table in the window and began the evaluation. Chunks of icy strawberries lingered in her mouth as the creamy flavor melted on her tongue. It was delicious. The waffle cone was fresh and crispy, and she had to fight the nagging urge to order another one. Ice cream was definitely heaven's food—or hell's temptation—and she was its tester.

Theresa watched the people who passed by the window and tried to determine who was a tourist and who was local. Some stood just a few feet from her, chatting with an animated, soundless enthusiasm on the other side of the glass. Others stopped, looking up and down the street, as if waiting for directions, or inspiration, on which way to go. She noticed that many of the cars were expensive or classic models, with license plates from Massachusetts or Connecticut. Perhaps Cape Cod was exclusively the playground of the Northeast—and of the privileged.

It suddenly dawned on Theresa that she didn't know a single person here. She was an outsider, a visitor, like the tiny wandering sea creatures she'd seen at the Aquarium that crawl into empty shells left behind. She had no experience in travel, in adapting to new places. The beautiful shell she'd been given was not her choice, and it had not been washed clean of its former occupant. It might not fit. Like Gypsy, she was being let out of the space she knew and given freedom she didn't even know she lacked.

Theresa picked up her sealed package and headed back to the car. She felt disconnected and lonely. All around her spring was announcing its arrival in bursting buds and trees with new leaves the color of delicate green lace. She climbed into the Jeep, closed the door and locked it. Eagerly, she broke the seal on the box and lifted out several small boxes and a handful of letters.

Her curiosity led her first to the velvety jewelry boxes. Inside she found gorgeous pearls, a diamond and ruby ring, and a large pin with swirls of sapphires and diamonds in the shape of a flower. Another box held a huge solitaire diamond ring and a ring with diamonds all around the band. Theresa slipped the diamond band on her finger, wondering whether it had been her grandmother's wedding ring.

The last box was a plain white box made of cardboard. It was lined with cottony puffs, as if cradling something extremely delicate or breakable. Theresa gently poked a finger in and found a note: "Here's a Glory-of-the-Seas treasure for my land treasure. With love, Stormy." At the bottom of the box was a seashell. Its elegant lines curved gracefully in a spiral coil at one end, the other end tapering off to seal the opening. It was about five inches long, a rusty orange color, splashed with dabs of yellow. Or maybe it was really a yellow shell with brownish patterns like a tightly wrapped net. Either way, it was wonderful to look at and to hold. It had been caressed by a thousand waves, given by someone with great love, and now was carefully protected with Grandmother's valuables.

The jewelry was breathtaking and expensive, but Theresa sat staring at the long shell and could not put it down. She wondered where it had come from and who Stormy was. The mystery of the giver could not be solved just then, but information about the shell would certainly be available at the public library. She would begin her learning about the ocean with a lesson on shells.

The library was farther down Main Street, and Theresa packed up the box again, careful to keep the letters together. She wanted time to read them in a quiet place when she would not be distracted, and she was already wondering whether two weeks would be enough time to sift through all the mementos and questions she was finding.

"Good afternoon," the woman at the front desk said, looking up from stamping books. "How may I help you?" she asked, as if she really meant it.

"I'm looking for reference books on shells. Something with identification pictures."

Theresa noticed the woman's name tag. It said, "Need help? Ask Ana." The name was written in calligraphy, and its spelling prompted Theresa to ask about the nationality.

"Portuguese," she replied. "My ancestors came here several generations ago, and I'm still here. Never even been off Cape."

"Not even to Boston?" Theresa asked, incredulously.

"No. We live quietly and have everything we need right here. I like to stay pretty close to home." Ana showed her where the reference books were kept and pointed to several large ones on the shelf.

Theresa noticed the woman did not wear a wedding ring but decided she was already getting a little too personal to pursue the family history. "Thanks for your help," she said, unable to call a woman so much older than she was by her first name. "I'll come back if I get stuck."

"I'll be here," replied Ana, genuinely. "You'll find lots of books on the ocean and marine life."

Theresa was fascinated by the pictures of beautiful shells from waters around the world. She read the descriptions and tried the Latin names. She traced some of the shapes with her finger. The colorful bumps and spikes and ridges, so smooth on the page, were plucked from a palette of nature's colors. No human could put together such combinations, she thought.

Her grandmother's shell sat on the table in front of her, and she occasionally looked up to compare it with a picture. She was amazed at the diversity and the similarities, but none quite matched the shell in front of her. Finally, in a book about highly collectible shells, she found "Glory-of-the-Seas" in the index. Her fingers fumbled to the page, and there it was—as beautiful and perfect as her grandmother's. "Considered one of the most valuable at auctions. Expect to pay at least a thousand dollars.

Very rare. Found mostly in museums."

She went on to read that Glory-of-the-Seas is found in the southwest Pacific, around the Philippines and Indonesia. *Not exactly a Cape Cod native!* "It has long been associated with romance and intrigue, theft and deceit, and is highly sought after by serious collectors." As Theresa reached to put a protective hand around the shell, she saw Ana standing nearby watching her, her face drained of color.

Theresa stood up, awkwardly clutching the shell. She wanted to tell Ana she'd been successful in her research, but the woman was gone.

CHAPTER SIX

Theresa debated the wisdom of disturbing Kevin at his office, of having personal conversation during business hours. She was not trying to burn her bridges, at least not yet consciously. Their communication was increasingly a minefield of emotions, but stalemate allowed neither party to forgive. She wanted to keep trying.

"Do you have a minute?" she asked, holding the phone with one hand and rubbing Gypsy's neck with the other.

"You bet. I'm trying to rewrite this brief, but it's just not coming together. The client is stressed, and we are all working long hours. Everything okay with you?"

"Everything is fine. Would you rather I call you at home tonight?"

"No, this is great. I miss you, Theresa. What's the word from Whimsy Towers?"

"Well, I ventured into town today and got the things from Grandmother's safe deposit box. Seems she valued a seashell from somebody named Stormy as much as some incredible jewelry that must have come from Grandfather. Or maybe other men in her life came bearing gifts."

"No other clues?"

"Not so far, but there are some letters that I'm about to read. I'm both excited and apprehensive about what I may learn, and I want to sit in the sunshine at Whimsy

Towers and let the truth unfold. My family seems to reveal itself in print better than in person!"

Kevin laughed. "Have you been to the beach?"

"I haven't actually been on it yet. Thought I'd take Gypsy for a beach walk this afternoon." She decided not to mention her discovery in the boathouse. Kevin would worry, and she didn't want to alarm him with uncertain news.

"I could use a long walk on a beach. Sounds wonderful. And the towers?"

"Oh, yes, the towers! Amazing! They have lights in them like lighthouses. One green and one red."

"Green and red? Your grandmother must have thought she lived on a boat! Sounds like the adventure rolls on, Theresa."

"Yes, I'm settling in and finding my way around the place. The weather is beautiful, and spring is just beginning to show off. Everything all right at home?"

"The house is too quiet without my girls. I'll probably work late here tonight. The finish line is almost in sight on this case. Maybe I could fly up and join you next weekend. I know we need to talk."

Theresa did not immediately answer. "Well, let's see," she replied, not sure whether she was ready to include him.

Was she searching for the family she didn't know or trying to dispose of the one she did? Her hesitancy was obvious. She sensed that Kevin didn't want to push her over the edge and didn't know how to catch her before she slipped.

The dog was safe territory. "Gypsy doing okay?" he asked.

"She seems fine, a happy mix of curiosity and contentment. There's lots of room to run and sniff. I think we'll have some outside relax time this afternoon. I'm anxious to get into the letters. Do you remember my father ever talking about a Claude or Stormy?"

"No, but Cape Cod was a closed door; we knew not to try to open it. Maybe the letters will help."

"Maybe," replied Theresa, looking down at the new diamond band on her right hand. "I'll let you know."

She hung up the phone and held her two hands out in front of her. Her plain gold wedding band was the only jewelry she wore. They had been married too quickly to worry about an engagement ring, and it seemed silly to buy one after the wedding. She always thought of the white roses as engagement flowers. Theresa smiled at the thought of Kevin nervously waiting for her with an armful of flowers and a heart full of anxious love. They had jumped into marriage with the optimism of youth.

Now she had jewelry from her grandmother's marriage, but that union, too, lacked sparkle, and the glitter of diamonds could not fix it. She wondered why Kevin never bought her jewelry. They exchanged gifts that were practical and predictable, with little risk of disappointment. They usually knew exactly what was coming, and the unwrapping was just a formality.

Theresa picked up the packet of letters and stepped

out onto the porch. Gypsy didn't wait to be called; an open door was all the invitation she needed. The dog ran ahead out onto the lawn, and Theresa sat down on the steps. The first letter, addressed to her grandmother, had never even been opened. She recognized the handwriting immediately and slid her finger under the flap to break the seal.

Dear Theodosia,

We have found a house in a nice neighborhood with big trees and a school nearby. Theresa watches the children walking with their mothers to school and asks me if Mommy will come back before she starts kindergarten. We both struggle to find our way here, even after two years. I am able to write copy at home for the ad agency where I work, and I'm glad for the time with Theresa. She often cries at night from bad dreams, and I'm afraid Emily is beginning to mingle with other faces and people in her young mind. I do not know how or if to hold onto the memory of a mother she will never know.

When I called today and you did not know who I was, tears of loss and anger welled up in me. Your softened voice, now empty of remembering, is like a distant echo of our happy days together as a family. Perhaps I just ran away, like a confused child who wants to hide from reality. I am so sorry, so very sorry, for the pain of our parting.

You are in good hands with your nurse. If you are able to understand this letter, please know that I love you and will be forever grateful for having your beautiful daughter in my life,

Tim

Inside the envelope was a photograph of a smiling Theresa. She was dressed in a navy blue coat with white trim and a little straw hat with flowers on top. She looked to be about three or four and stood proudly holding an Easter basket full of colored eggs. Theresa read the letter again. She could not imagine her father running away from anything; he had been her rock.

Sitting in the warm sunshine, Theresa looked out across the lawn towards the water and realized that she, too, was running, looking for escape from a situation she did not know how to handle. And she smiled at the ironic thought that her flight had brought her back to the beginning, back to the place that began the journey.

The afternoon sky was gray blue, with wisps of white clouds separating it from the blue gray ocean. Theresa reflected on how nature's elements come together at the horizon, always out of touch and distant. They do not argue where they meet; the storms occur before that faraway, closing line.

She watched sailboats of varying sizes skim across the water and wondered whether she would like sailing. The boats often turned sharply to catch a breeze, and some had brightly colored sails in front that looked like puffed trumpeters leading into the wind. Her mother had been an excellent sailor, but she didn't know whether her father had ever tried it again after his wife's death. Until the letter he'd left her, with the details of her mother's accident, Theresa had never known her family's connection to sailing and the fury of the ocean.

Looking out on the scene of leisure and sport, she squinted in the bright sun. No hint of danger lurked, no threat of harm, no dark cloud. The water was a friend to fun, she thought, and she gazed absently at the waves licking the shoreline like a persistent mother cat cleaning her kitten. Looking back at the pile of letters in her lap, she picked up the next one and stared at it.

The date stamped on the front of the envelope was October 31, 1929. Theresa rarely wrote letters herself and realized how lazy the convenience of telephoning had made her. It took patience and organization to sit down and write a letter. Words had to be chosen that could sit awhile on the page and be reread without regret. Perhaps she would write Kevin a letter, she thought.

The handwriting was bold, with the graceful flow of an old-fashioned fountain pen.

Dear Theodosia,

I am writing you with grave news and hope not to alarm you with any urgency in my voice or manner. The stock market has crashed to an unimaginable level, and my holdings are entirely lost. I am sure you have heard the radio reports and seen the news in the papers. The fall on Wall Street has driven some men to desperate measures. They are unable to face the future that seems to lie ahead.

We must try to be sensible and evaluate our position. It is necessary to trim all extra expenses and look toward the possibilities of rebuilding our assets. Without the dividends and sales from stocks, our income is greatly diminished. The law firm is stable, and my position is secure, although some employees will be released.

I see no way for you to remain in Cape Cod, and I will make temporary adjustments in my personal and social arrangements for your return to our house. It may be necessary to send Emily to a different school or to a nonboarding school when you are back in South Carolina. These changes need to be made to protect our family name and prospects.

Most sincerely, James

Theresa searched for answers to questions not asked: Was Whimsy Towers to be sold? Abandoned? Did Emily suddenly have more time with her parents? Had Grandfather been living with a mistress? She laughed at the suggestion of "temporary adjustments"!

And then she surprised herself by considering the possibility that Kevin might have an affair while she was out of town. Her imagination took off. He would not see it coming: An innocent invitation to have dinner with one of the secretaries after a long day in the office, a quick drink back at her apartment, her sympathetic ear to the problems of the day. Theresa pictured him sitting on a couch with a young woman in a short skirt, his arm relaxed along the top of the sofa, his brow furrowed from thoughts of work. She would melt into him, tentatively kissing him on the neck and cheek. Caught off guard, he might respond to her eagerness like a flattered and vulnerable man who ate the same dinner every night, hungry for variety but afraid of change.

Theresa knew Kevin was honest and honorable, but he was also a handsome and successful man. A wedding ring was no guarantee of fidelity. She had never seen him flirt with another woman, but their lovemaking had long since lost the thrill of forbidden pleasure. She yearned for that urgency of young love, not love as a condition of convenience frozen by responsibilities. Theresa was surprised that feelings of jealousy welled up, of not wanting to lose what was not quite enough. They knew each other's mind and body, the coming together of which brought familiarity instead of excitement.

"Routine," said Theresa aloud, "routine is the death of love."

She looked into the next envelope, trying to push the thoughts of Kevin with another woman out of her mind. She squirmed uneasily. *Could Kevin really be unfaithful?* She wondered whether he ever thought about other women. She wondered whether she could ask him. And then she wondered whether she herself could be tempted. Unconsciously, she fanned her face with the envelope. Thoughts of fantasy and sexual desire startled and aroused her, and she felt a need she was not used to feeling. She looked out across the lawn and imagined making love with Kevin on the warm grass.

Looking down at the letter in her hand, Theresa pulled her emotions back to the present. The handwriting was the same as the previous letter, and perhaps there would be answers to the layers of mystery in her grandparents' relationship.

November 19, 1929

Dear Theodosia,

Your letter pursues topics we had agreed not to discuss. For the sake of my position and the community, we must continue the appearance of a marriage. My reputation depends on it. There has never been divorce in the Hampton family, and I will not consider it.

We can have separate rooms. Be assured that my comforts are satisfied elsewhere, and there will be no demands on you. This is a time of great stress and upheaval, and it is necessary for you to do your part in the obligations of the moment. Sell the Cape Cod house for whatever price it will bring. Surely someone there can still afford to buy.

I have been looking for the jewelry that was my mother's. Especially the sapphire and diamond flower brooch. Do you have it in Massachusetts?

Your husband, James

The closing words were the summary of the whole letter for Theresa: "Your husband," your boss and master, the authority of rank and the audacity of power. Wives were not much more than possessions back then, she realized, but Theodosia was cut from a different bolt of fabric. And Whimsy Towers and the sapphire and diamond pin were safe in the hands of her granddaughter. Some plans were destined to fall off track.

The other papers were receipts for Oriental carpets, the real estate contract to purchase Whimsy Towers, and an appraisal of jewelry. The appraisal was dated December 11, 1929, and was typed on letterhead from a jeweler in Boston that read, "Specialists in Appraisal and Estate Jewelry." Theresa scanned the short list and was jolted by the last entry: "exquisite diamond and sapphire brooch—value $11,000.00." The details of stone arrangement, cut, and clarity followed, but Theresa was riveted by the value. Surely $11,000 could have bought quite a house in 1929—or settled a lot of bills! No wonder Grandfather was anxious to reel in the jewelry after Black Thursday.

Grandmother must have headed straight to Boston to find out for herself the value of her jewelry after receiving her husband's letter. The pearls were valued at $4,000, the diamond and ruby ring, at $4,500; and another ring of all sapphires, which wasn't in the box, was listed at $3,000. Theresa wondered what had happened to the sapphire ring, and then she shuddered to think that it might have gone to the bottom of the ocean as a gift on her mother's hand.

Handwritten at an angle across the bottom of the page were two more entries: "Solitaire diamond engagement ring, $5,500," and "wedding band with diamonds, $3,800." There was no indication of who had made the additional appraisals or when they were made, but Theresa could imagine her grandmother pulling off her wedding rings for the last time, establishing their value, and then sealing them up with other memories of her faraway husband. *What had finally transpired between them? How stubborn was this plucky Southern woman?*

Theresa was finding more questions than answers at Whimsy Towers. She whistled for Gypsy and headed down to the beach, deciding not to stop at the boathouse to check on further activity. Players from the past were filling her thoughts, and those in the present would have to wait.

Theresa kicked off her shoes and left them in the tall grass where green met sandy brown on a long stretch of quiet beach. She unbuttoned her blouse and let the wind blow through her, feeling the hot rays of the afternoon sun against her skin. No one was around to see her, and she closed her eyes to savor the salt air and calm.

Gypsy ran ahead, occasionally veering into the water, her tail wagging with a horizontal chop through the rising waves. When she lost her footing, she bobbed with the ease of a cork, legs paddling furiously toward the land, until the next wave gently and effortlessly carried her to firm ground. Theresa threw a stick over the dog's head into the ocean, and Gypsy instinctively charged forward to retrieve it.

"Not bad for a land dog." She laughed. "Guess your water retrieval skills are built in after all!" The stick did not make it all the way back to Theresa, but she was running down the beach, calling over her shoulder to

Gypsy, "Come on! I'll race you!"

The two ran along the edge of the water, where the sand was firm and moist. They were used to jogging together in Virginia, but the regular route was sidewalks near their house. When Gypsy was younger, Theresa could go several miles with her; now it was a combination of jogging and walking for just the distance around the block.

Accepting changes in life was what Theresa was grappling with, she decided. Knowing when to make a change, or take a stand, or turn away and ignore the whole situation. She thought of her father's last weeks. He had seemed troubled by something other than his illness but would not confide in her or in Kevin. He'd closed himself up in his house with his memories and his fears. He had seemed frail and exhausted. They had taken away his car keys and called or saw him every day. They had wondered how long he could stay alone in his house, but they'd avoided talking about it. The decision had eventually made itself.

Theresa thought about her grandmother's last thirty years at Whimsy Towers, not really knowing what was going on or who was with her, but at peace with being in her own home, in the atmosphere she loved. The same dedicated nurse had spent all those years as a companion and caregiver. She must have raised her son here, thought Theresa, and she wondered how the three lives had intertwined and how old the boy was.

Theresa looked back at the house and saw how it rose

from the land as the coastline pushed up from the water. It certainly stood as a beacon, if not a lighthouse, on the shore. The towers would be visible for quite a distance out into the ocean. The one on the right side, the red one, was above Grandmother's bedroom, and Theresa could picture her slowly climbing the steps at bedtime to take in the night sounds and air from the little balcony. She could have watched the rolling ocean and cursed the wind as it blew angry waves in tumbling curls over her lost daughter. Or perhaps the memory was washed from her ravaged mind and had slipped away like a soft breeze.

Farther down the beach, a neighbor's house came into view, tucked back into towering wild rose bushes and partially hidden by a wooden fence with pointed posts. No patio furniture or beach chairs or other sign of activity was evident. The tide had chewed into the shore, shortening the beach area and bringing the house much closer to the water's edge than Whimsy Towers. Theresa decided she would go that afternoon to buy an outdoor table with bright umbrella and some lawn chairs. She wanted to see life at Whimsy Towers.

Sandpipers and seagulls scurried in circles in front of her as Gypsy ran ahead. She thought of Grandmother's Glory-of-the-Seas and imagined the thrill of looking down and seeing such a shell lying on the beach. It probably was found by divers in deep waters, but sometimes wondrous treasures do get laid in full view in life's path.

For several hours Theresa wandered, sat, stood, and stared. The beach remained deserted. Her feet were cold from stepping into the still-icy chill of the water. Her winter-white toes pushed into the sand like anxious explorers, sinking and then pushing on. She wondered when it would be warm enough to swim comfortably, and she decided her Virginia-bred beach feet could use some waking up with red polish.

Enough daylight remained for another trip into town, and Theresa took the road that seemed to run parallel to the shore. A small Lawn and Garden Center with dozens of potted ferns along the roadside caught her attention, and she steered Red Rover into the parking lot, searching for signs of garden furniture. At the back fence she spotted a group of round tables, each with an umbrella coming up from the center. The open umbrella tops looked like giant-sized hard candy, with colorful stripes of pink and yellow, their edges bumping into each other. They were huddled together as if expecting to be sold as a unit, a dazzling tent over a summertime party. Theresa got out and began to look them over.

"Hello there," someone called from the jungle of ferns. "How can I help you today?"

Theresa turned to see a woman about her age, wearing blue jeans and a cable-knit sweater that hadn't seen its true color in some years. A long braid, tied with twine, flopped down her back.

"Hi. I'm looking for a table and chairs. Looks like you have quite a few."

"Yes, we've been stocking up for the season. The rush begins in another ten days or so. You've come at just the right time. What kind are you looking for?"

"Well, I guess I don't really know," said Theresa, realizing she had never bought outdoor furniture. Their porch at home had all wicker, and it did not get wet unless a peculiar wind swept rain through the screen on the northwest side. "What do you recommend?"

"Covered or uncovered?"

"Uncovered, I think. I want to put it right out in the middle of the lawn."

"I'd stay away from cushions then. Some are designed not to absorb rain, but they do get a little flat. And mind the color you choose because of fading in bright light. Chemicals can only fight Mother Nature so far!"

The woman took long strides toward the huddled tables, pulling them apart to make room for Theresa to walk around. They were clean and new; the umbrellas smelled faintly of dye and packaging. *Fresh beginnings.*

"I think I'll take this one," said Theresa, pointing to a white table with yellow and white umbrella. "Yellow is sunshine's color. There should be no fighting!"

Both women laughed, and Theresa helped pull the table out from the pack.

"Hey, Rick! We need a little help here," yelled the woman to a man piling bags of mulch or dirt. He stood up and looked in their direction but did not move. The two women had already separated out the table.

"Do you need delivery?" she asked Theresa. "No charge if you're local."

"I guess I do," answered Theresa, liking the sound of

being "local." "I don't think a table and four chairs would quite fit in my Jeep."

"We can bring it first thing in the morning. Where do you live?"

Theresa gave her the address and directions. As she turned to leave, she noticed Rick loading the heavy bags into an old Dodge Ram truck. The tailgate was down, and she could see rakes, shovels, a bird bath base, and a jumble of bricks. The truck was parked next to a shiny new Dodge truck, with extended cab and green lettering on the side that read, "Lawn and Garden Center, Our Family Serving Yours."

The silvery ram's head jutting out of the hood of the old truck caught her eye, and she called out, "Great truck. I like your ram."

As soon as she'd said it, she felt foolish and pointed awkwardly to the hood ornament on the older truck.

"Oh, yeah, thanks. At first I didn't like it, but now I've gotten kinda used to it. Like a bowsprit that points the way. Maybe someday it will be a collector's item." He laughed.

Theresa fantasized what the ram would look like on the front of Red Rover. Cars and trucks were becoming so ordinary, she thought, having no room for frivolous ornaments with the new aerodynamic designs. She had seen customized cars whose owners had incorporated incongruous elements, creating vehicles that were true only to their makers' imaginations. Thank goodness for dreamers, she thought. They're the ones who really change the course of things. *Most people just march along the side of the road.*

Rick's shirt was dirty in front from lifting the bags close to his chest. He was tall and rugged, already suntanned so early in the season. He stood waiting before starting back to his work, as if to see whether Theresa would continue. She liked these two people and lingered for a moment, deciding whether to look around for some plants. She was glad to have met a couple her age.

"Do you sell lilacs?" she asked.

"Yes, we do," he replied, pulling off a glove and coming toward her. "This dwarf variety is particularly good. It's called 'Miss Kim.'" He rubbed several leaves between his fingers, as if enjoying the feel of the smooth leaf. It was too early for blossoms from the tiny buds. "Plant some near a porch or open window, and you'll feel absolutely intoxicated with sweet fragrance. Guaranteed."

Theresa laughed. "I'm not sure I want to lose control of myself under horticultural influence! But I'll try five or six. Let's say six. Will they fit on the truck with the table?"

"Oh, sure. No problem. Do you need peat moss and mulch?"

"Yes, I think I'd better be prepared. I don't know about the soil here."

"That should do it," he said. "And we can just add it to your ticket. Anything else?"

"No, thanks. I'd better not get too far ahead of myself!"

Theresa turned to go back into the little office to revise her purchase charge. At the door she passed a rack of brochures with local information about sightseeing, shops, and restaurants. She stopped to look. A lecture series on coastal ecology, a seafood festival, and several pamphlets about whale watching particularly interested her.

"Can you see whales in Chatham?" she asked the girl at the counter, who looked like an almost-teenage version of the woman outside.

"Not really. The whale watching boats operate mostly out of Provincetown. That's the best place to go. And the closest. Are you here for long?"

"Just a few weeks, I think."

"Well, there are trips around Nantucket and the Vineyard that are excellent for whale watching as well as seeing the area. You need to plan a whole day, however, not just a couple of hours. Have you ever seen a real whale?"

"No, this is all new to me, and I want to take it all in."

"You'll love it. It's amazing. It's almost unbelievable the first time you see this enormous animal come to the surface like a rising mountain. The Dolphin Fleet has scientists onboard that tell you all about the whales and dolphins and birds. They really want to protect these creatures and educate people about them. It's so neat! Take a warm sweater when you go, though; it gets colder out on the water."

"Thanks for the tip. How far is Provincetown?" asked Theresa.

"From here, less than an hour. It's a … an interesting community. Lots of galleries and fishing boats and good restaurants."

"I think you've just planned my day for tomorrow. Thanks," said Theresa, tucking the brochures into her purse.

"You're welcome. Have a great time. But don't forget about your delivery in the morning. The bushes will wait for you to plant them; just don't let them dry out."

"I promise," she replied, as she stepped back outside and headed for her car. The couple were busy stacking bags together, laughing and talking. Theresa envied them. Rick stopped and waved, and she waved back with a smile. Chatham was a neighborly kind of place, she decided.

"See you tomorrow," he called, giving a playful pull to the long brown braid that swished across his arm.

CHAPTER SEVEN

The potholes in the driveway to Whimsy Towers had not changed in two days, but Theresa drove around them with the assurance of knowing what lay ahead. She remembered her first glimpse of the house, with its bold pink trim and odd towers, and her approach this time held a mixture of eagerness and ease. There was no curiosity. There is no surprise in coming home to the place that holds your heart, and she felt a sense of welcome and belonging.

Evening was slowly dropping its misty veil, and sounds of crickets and mournful bird calls signaled the end of day. Theresa stopped the car in the thicket of trees and opened all the windows. She put her head back and closed her eyes. Squirrels scampered up and down tree trunks, and dry leaves on the ground crunched with small animals hurrying home for safety and rest. Night would soon take over.

And with the daylight yielding to darkness, Theresa wanted to get back to the house. She was anxious to resolve the puzzle of the lights in the towers. *How could she turn them on? Were they still connected?* It would be easier to see their effect at night, and she was determined to see Whimsy Towers in full glow.

Gypsy was waiting inside the kitchen. The Jeep was

not yet a familiar sound, and Theresa could hear cautionary barks as Red Rover got near the house. Coming into full view, Theresa could see an excited dog in the window, running to the door and back again. All was well.

"Hi, Gypsy. Did you miss me?" Theresa called as she opened the screen door. "We have some detective work to do."

The dog continued wagging her tail, with mute acceptance of whatever was to come. Perhaps the gift of language was a hindrance to relationships. Theresa laughed to herself and kneeled down to hug her devoted pet. *Can people develop unconditional love?* Communication through words could twist intent and shift the foundation of trust. She never had to worry that Gypsy was in a bad mood or had misinterpreted something she had said. Eat, sleep, give love, and be loved—simple ingredients for a full and satisfying life.

"Who said, 'it's a dog's life'?" She laughed aloud, rubbing Gypsy's neck enthusiastically. Her furry companion dusted the floor with brisk, sweeping strokes of her wagging tail. "You've got it made, sweet girl," Theresa pronounced, with a final pat. "Now let's see about a light show. We could have the ultimate in Christmas lights!"

She tried several wall switches, flicking each with the hope that the tower lights might come on, but instead, different parts of rooms lit up. Several switches brought no response, inside or out, but each time she still checked outdoors for a glimmer of red or green.

Finally, they headed upstairs to Grandmother's bedroom. Theresa realized that she should stop thinking of it as her grandmother's room and accept the transition from the past. "Thank you, Grandmother," she said, as she entered the yellow room and surveyed again the paintings and antiques and knickknack memories. "I love your house, and I'm sorry I could not be here for you; I just didn't know." She sighed deeply, taking in the details of the room.

Branches from the tall oak tree tapped against the window, as if trying to get her attention, and as she glanced in the direction of the beckoning sound, she saw a switch above the far bedside table. "Bingo!" she said, moving towards the bed.

She turned the switch while looking out the windows facing the ocean. The evening sky was transformed from a dusky haze punctuated by stars to the glow of a million colored flashlights pointing heavenward. Sky and earth fused in the hue of awakened darkness. She strained her eyes to see the water, but, like a mirror, it reflected back the lights of Whimsy Towers. All celestial competition was subdued, and the moon gave up like a ghost.

Theresa ran down the stairs and through the house. Gypsy followed close behind and barely made it through the screen door as Theresa hurried out onto the lawn. She ran about fifty feet before stopping to catch her breath and turning towards the house.

"Wow!" she exclaimed. "Incredible! Grandmother, what in the world is this about?"

Gypsy made a few staccato barks to register her participation in the excitement, and Theresa stood looking at the two brightly-lit towers in stunned silence.

The tower on the right side, the one painted red above her grandmother's bedroom, beamed out the red light; the green tower, the green light. The lights did not blink or rotate; they were focused straight toward the ocean, piercing the darkness with single-minded pursuit. The sides of the light casings in the towers blocked any sideways distraction or beams, and the house sat perched like a space ship awaiting visitors from the deep.

"Let's leave them on awhile," she said to Gypsy. "We'll let Whimsy Towers strut her stuff for tonight. The old girl is back in business!"

Several weeks would pass before Theresa discovered true meaning in that statement, but the lights stayed on all night, and she slept soundly with the soft glow of red and green filling her yellow bedroom.

It was Gypsy who first heard the sound of someone driving toward the house. The long driveway provided ample opportunity to see advancing cars after they cleared the wooded area, but the ocean could muffle the sound of an engine and the crunch of gravel if the waves were kicking up. Theresa had let the dog out and then returned to bed with a cup of coffee and a book about gardening. Gypsy stayed close to the porch, lying in the grass and snoring contentedly, with the morning sun soothing her slightly plump body. Occasionally, her front paws jerked in an odd motion, as if she were trying to run while lying sideways.

Perhaps she felt the truck's movement through the ground, or perhaps her protective sense never quite fell asleep, but long before the shiny truck with green lettering arrived at the corner of the house, she was on her feet and barking.

"What is it, Gypsy?" called Theresa from the window, unable to see the truck from her angle. "What's up?"

Three short honks reminded Theresa of her delivery, and she left her coffee behind as she grabbed her robe.

The man called Rick was still sitting in the truck when she arrived on the scene. Gypsy had stopped barking, and he was talking to her through the open truck window. Her tail wagged tentatively.

"Good morning," he called. "Sorry if I'm too early. Guess I should have called."

"Oh, no, you're fine. I just don't seem to pay much attention to the time here. It's such a beautiful morning to relax and enjoy."

"I'm not sure your dog shares in that!" He laughed. "Can I get out?"

Theresa approached the truck and stood next to Gypsy. Her eyes were almost level with Rick's as he sat behind the wheel. His light brown hair was tousled and bleached in front from the sun; a small twig was caught in a curl over his ear, and she resisted the urge to pluck it out. He had on a clean shirt for the new day, and she could smell the lemony scent of shaving cream or aftershave. Embarrassed by her observations, she backed up a step.

"Oh sure," she replied. "Just say her name, and she'll lick you to death. It's Gypsy."

The door opened, and Rick stepped out, with his hand extended to the dog. "Come here, Gypsy," he said. "Come here, you noisy old girl. Where'd you get the energy for all that barking?"

Gypsy eagerly accepted the attention and petting and gave approving sniffs to man and truck. She was quick to expand her circle of acquaintance.

"Shameful!" Theresa laughed. "Jack the Ripper could give you a biscuit or a pet and you'd welcome him right in! So much for my security system."

"I think your system is okay. She did bark and wait to see what I would do. Most men would not take a chance with a loose dog, especially a big one. And I don't think you have to worry much around here, unless you're expecting some unsavory visitors."

Theresa's thoughts raced back to the boathouse and the bits of food left at her doorstep. "I hope you're right. By the way, I'm Theresa."

"I know. I have the ticket, remember?" A huge, Cheshire-cat smile slowly formed on his face, showing beautiful white teeth, and his blue eyes sparkled with relaxed mischief. "I'm Rick."

His eyes were even bluer than Kevin's, and she wanted to ask him whether he wore contact lenses. "Yes, I remember from last night."

"Are you the new owner here?" he asked.

"Is that a condition for delivery?"

"No, no, I just wondered. I used to take care of this place for the bank. I love it here; it's so private, and the view is wonderful. I'd come do the work and then sit and read or do crosswords. It's lucky they didn't pay me by the hour! My contract was for weekly maintenance, but during the summer and vacations, I would pop over for a couple hours' peace at sunset or to watch the geese migrating. This property is a hidden treasure."

"Did you know my grandmother?" Theresa blurted out, hardly believing she was talking to a direct link to her past.

"You don't mean the lady with her son?"

"No, an older lady. The woman you're talking about was her nurse and companion."

"No, when the bank hired me, the nurse was about to move out and leave the place empty. She and her son had taken care of the yard and things, I guess, for many years. She told me they always had repairs made immediately and tried to keep everything in good order. These old houses can be a money pit, especially if they get behind in maintenance. I got the feeling it was hard for her to leave."

Theresa was silent.

"Are you here for long?" he continued.

"Long enough to plant these bushes and enjoy my new table," she answered, pulling her robe together as it started to slip open. "I inherited the house and have just come up from Virginia to see the Cape."

"For the first time?"

"More or less," she answered, deciding not to go into the story of her childhood over bagged lilacs and mulch.

He accepted her answer and did not pursue the subject.

"Do you have garden tools? Like a basic shovel?"

Theresa laughed. "I really don't know! I hadn't thought about it. Maybe in the cellar."

"Tell you what," he continued. "How about I lend a hand in planting these for you? I have a shovel and a little extra time before picking up my next job. We'll call it 'on the house'—or maybe in exchange for a cup of coffee."

"That's a deal I can't refuse," she replied, liking the look in his blue eyes and holding out her hand to seal the bargain. His grip was firm, not the wishy-washy kind of limp handshake that many men offer women. They lingered for just a moment longer than required for the business at hand, their hands and eyes locked together; and her robe slipped open again with the shaking of her arm.

"Thanks," she stuttered, grabbing at the robe with her free hand. "I think I'll just change my clothes real fast and bring you that coffee."

"Sounds great. I'll start unloading." Rick smiled and watched her as she headed back into the house. She felt his gaze following her, but she didn't want to turn and acknowledge it. She didn't want to feel curious about this man, and if truth be told, she didn't want him seeing her looking so unkempt.

"Where do you want the bushes?" he called, as she was

halfway up the steps.

Without hesitating, she looked back at him and answered, "Along the porch. Remember your promise about the intoxicating fragrance?"

"Consider it done," he replied, bending forward in a deep, comical bow as Theresa reached for the screen door.

Fifteen minutes passed before she emerged from the house, carrying two cups of coffee. She had debated taking time to shower and wash her hair; it dried quickly with a rub of the towel, but instead she squeezed almond mousse on it and ran her fingers through the soft curls, pulling on them to add body.

She'd tried on several outfits; one looked too fussy and the others too drab. And then she chastised herself for caring what she wore while a man muddied himself for a cup of coffee and some pleasant conversation. The clothes piled up on her bed, and she slipped into a comfortable pair of old jeans and a tired T-shirt.

"'Vanity, vanity. All is vanity,'" she sighed as she passed the hall mirror and stopped to decide if she should add a touch of lipstick. "Bushes, Theresa. For heaven's sake, you're just planting bushes!"

She skipped down the stairs, following the fragrant trail of fresh-brewed coffee. She loved this kitchen; it didn't take itself too seriously. There were no long expanses of counter tops holding gadgety equipment that never got used—or appliances so clean and shiny that no one had obviously ever turned them on, or cared to. This kitchen had heart. It had paintings and drawings and color and carpets. It sang out with cozy welcome and an invitation to sit and feel the wonder of the place.

Theresa poured strong coffee into mugs embossed with tropical fish. The steamy aroma of roasted hazelnuts filled the kitchen, and she wished the fresh coffee smell would cling to her like perfume. It was bold and inviting, and Theresa felt the tingle of a bright Cape Cod morning and the new beginnings of friendship and exploration.

"Cream and sugar?" she called, pushing the screen door open with her hip.

"No thanks, just black."

"You're easy," she answered, instantly wishing she'd chosen a different word.

"I don't want to miss the flavor of the bean," he joked. "Besides, it's just less bother."

"Well, this bean is pretty strong. Let me know if it's too much. I do have milk. The cupboard is stocked up." She wondered if "less bother" was appropriate only for the moment or if it was his style in general.

She handed him the fish mug, and a wedding ring sparkled in the light as he pulled off his left glove and took it from her. She turned her eyes away, looking toward the water. Crows screamed from the trees behind the house. The new table sat on the grassy lawn, its umbrella closed and tied like an upturned fist.

"That looks great there," she said, without much enthusiasm.

"I didn't know if you wanted it closer to the house or

to the water. We can carry it either way."

Rick sipped his coffee and watched Theresa as she stared out at the ocean. The morning tide brought a softness to the roll of the waves. Their edges curled over with a silvery flicker, and seagulls rode the gentle crests.

"I think it's just perfect right there. Do you have time to sit a minute?" she asked.

Rick looked at his watch and then at the four holes he'd dug next to the porch. "I think I'm allowed a coffee break." He smiled.

"I really appreciate your help, Rick. This is above and beyond the call of duty or the meaning of service. You've created a devoted customer."

"That's our aim—service with a smile. My parents started the business with that motto many years ago. And I told you how much I love coming here. But don't worry; now that I know the place is occupied, I won't drop in. Besides, your ferocious dog might attack me."

Gypsy lay close to the truck, her side heaving with deep sleep.

Theresa laughed and said, "Yes, she is a mean, man-eating thing." She wanted to say, "Please come back anytime," but that did not seem a very appropriate invitation to a married man—or from a married woman. She remembered the bank trustee telling her that Rick had lost his wife a few years back, and she wondered how soon he had remarried. He seemed relaxed and happy.

"I understand you teach at the community college," she began.

"Wow, you do have some unexpected information."

"The bank gave me your name and number and thought I might like to call you about taking care of the house. I didn't realize last night that you were the same Rick."

"Will you be living here alone?" he asked, looking down at his coffee.

"I ... I'm not sure exactly. My plan is to stay a few weeks and think some things through. I live in Virginia."

"What do you do there?" he asked, bringing his eyes up to meet hers.

"I write children's books and do illustrations. I always loved to doodle and draw, and one day I found myself writing stories to go with the pictures, and people started paying me for them. It's a career that I created by mistake; there was no plan. I love it, though, and I can set my own schedule and work at home."

"Then why not work here?" asked Rick.

Theresa fidgeted in her chair, unconsciously twisting her wedding ring around on her finger. She was ashamed of herself for not wanting to tell him that she had a husband and a life that were expecting her back. *Uncertainty was choking her.* She liked this new place and the new feelings that were coming with it, and she was not ready to confront the decisions that waited.

"It's not that easy," she replied.

"Do you have children?" he asked.

"No, no children. But I do have a husband and a house and a mortgage and responsibilities." She sighed and stared at the distant horizon, where blue met blue.

"I'm sorry. I didn't mean to . . . "

"No, it's all right," she interrupted, smiling at him with the sun on her face. "I just have to sort through some changes in my life and see what's important. Do you ever feel tossed into a situation and unable to decide where to go next?"

As soon as she'd said it, she felt foolish and insensitive, remembering what she had been told about his past; but she continued before he could speak. "It's just that sometimes, when life throws painful surprises at us, it's hard to regain one's footing and continue. The path is no longer so certain and clear as it had been."

Rick was silent for moment. "Theresa, I can only say that hurt does heal. Change does make us stronger, and as trite as it sounds, life moves on. We grow. Each day is an opportunity to prove it. Each day that beautiful sun rises again." He lifted his face toward the rays of sun climbing to midday. They sat quietly, absorbed in the warmth of memories and the maze of choices and chance, loss and new beginnings.

"Guess I better get digging," started Rick. "Two more holes and then I'll get the bushes in. I'd like to water them down before it's too hot."

His voice startled and comforted her at the same time. She was happy just sitting there with him, just listening to the waves and the birds and the reassurance that life was a challenge that she could master. The death of loved ones brought hearts together to grieve and rebuild. She wanted to love life, she determined; more than anything else, she wanted to love life.

Gypsy awoke as Rick hauled the first of the lilac bushes off the back of the truck. She stretched and quivered and then curled up to resume her sleep. Theresa came over to help unload, smiling at the dog lying in the direct path of work. "Great spot," she said to deaf ears.

The bushes were not too heavy, and she carried them to the holes that Rick was filling with peat moss and loose dirt.

"The soil is really good here," he said. "You should be able to have a great garden, if you want. Are you a gardener?"

"I do like to dig in the dirt." She laughed. "I tend to go for perennials and easy care plants, however. And I hesitate to commit to a garden here. It would just create more for you to look after when I go." She stopped for a moment. "I do want to talk with you about some maintenance arrangement, if you're willing."

Rick looked up at her from his crouched position, and Theresa felt like a country girl, fresh from the field. The morning sun cast golden shadows on her dark hair, and her shirt and jeans were brushed with dirt.

"Let's sit down and figure out what you need. I've got to get going now, but I can come back when it's convenient for you."

He carefully spread mulch around the last bush and instructed her to let the hose trickle on each one for ten minutes.

"I guess we've got each other's phone number," he said, somewhat sheepishly. "We need to figure out a maintenance schedule that you're comfortable with. If we keep selling you more plants, I'll create business two ways!" He laughed as he climbed into the truck.

Gypsy reluctantly got up as the engine started and the truck began to move.

"Thanks again, Rick, for all your help," Theresa said. "And thank your wife for helping me select the table. I really love it."

"You're welcome, Theresa. I'm glad I could help. I hope you'll like Chatham." And as he started down the drive, he leaned out the window and called over his shoulder, with that broad grin, "She's my sister."

CHAPTER EIGHT

Almost a week passed before Theresa thought again about whale watching. The breezy and bright mornings seduced her into staying at Whimsy Towers. She sat for hours under the umbrella at her new table, sometimes with her legs outstretched on an adjacent chair to get some sun and sometimes criss-crossed in Indian posture. She read and drew and listened to her thoughts. Gypsy wandered around the property, never going out of sight and checking often to see whether Theresa had moved; she didn't want to miss the cue for a beach walk.

Rick had not called to talk about a work schedule, and she was too embarrassed by their parting conversation to call him. But the grass was getting long, and either she needed to buy a lawn mower or she needed to make some arrangement. The prospect of serious yard work was not appealing, and she felt grateful that Kevin always cared for the lawn at home. She wondered for the first time whether he actually enjoyed it or did it simply from duty or habit. He fertilized, mulched, and mowed; she was free to design flower beds and plant what she wanted. Not exactly a fair division, if labor and pleasure were the ingredients of a yard.

Theresa realized she'd been staying around the house in part because she was curious about Rick. She hoped he'd call. *Was he really married after all? Or did he wear a wedding ring from a wife he'd lost and couldn't quite let go of?* She thought of her father and wondered whether he'd worn a ring while her mother was alive. When he died, the only jewelry she'd found in his house was a pair of gold cuff links with his engraved initials.

Leaving the shady cool of the umbrella, Theresa went into the house and dialed the number taped to the phone. An answering machine came on.

"Hello. Sorry not to be here to take your call. Please leave a message and a phone number after the beep."

Theresa took a deep breath and held it. She considered hanging up and then exhaled as she spoke.

"Hi," she began slowly, stretching out the vowel sound while she debated what to say next. "This message is for Rick. It's Theresa calling. I just wondered when it might be convenient to discuss the work around my house we talked about when you were here." She hesitated, as if he was going to respond. "I'm sure you are busy, but I'll need hip boots before long to get through this grass." She stopped, thinking she sounded a little too presumptuous and corny. "We could deal with this over the phone, and you wouldn't need to come back." Pausing again, trying to think of a businesslike way to wrap up this rambling, she continued, "I'm headed to Provincetown this afternoon. You have the number. Thanks. Bye."

She hung up the phone, wishing she could erase her words and start over. She was frustrated that the answering machine gave no hint of who else might hear her message. But most of all, she realized, she wanted to call back again, just to hear the sound of Rick's voice on the tape.

"Get a grip, Theresa," she said to herself. "You've had too much salt air!"

She closed her eyes, put her hands to her temples, and shook her head. The curls in her hair had tightened from the moist ocean breeze, and she felt them bounce with untamed freedom. She couldn't remember whether she had brushed her hair that morning—or the morning before. Living alone with sun, sand, and water had reduced her to nature's child, without worrying about makeup or tidy hair or even covering all the parts of her body that polite society required.

Whimsy Towers had cast its spell on her; she felt no desire to be anywhere else. The absence of routine and responsibility, of time itself, allowed her to eat, sleep, wander, and read on her own schedule. It was luxury loaded with selfishness, she realized; but like the waves creeping up the beach, days repeated with gentle changes that soothed and charmed her. No storms had yet ravaged the shore.

Grandmother had come to this place and never left. Leaving behind her husband and all the obligations of her social position, she had begun a new life. She had traded the South for the North and the security of old friendships for new ones. Grandmother did not sit still, Theresa decided. A dining room that seats a dozen people does not suggest a lonesome woman who ran away from the world.

Theresa wondered whether she could ever leave Kevin, whether her life would be better or just different without him. *What is the tipping point that leads to change?* For Theodosia Hampton, there was Paris—and a pregnancy outside her marriage. Was she a rebel in hoop skirts, a southern belle reacting against what was expected of her? Perhaps there have always been women wandering the marital maze of searching and belonging.

The 1920s had been filled with new opportunities for women. They were on the brink of social revolution that would rock the country's bedrooms and bank accounts. Women wanted choices. Theresa pictured her grandmother before her marriage in the '20s as a suffragette, carrying a sign demanding the right to vote, her chestnut hair piled properly on top of her head or perhaps streaming down her back in subtle defiance. Causes were good, Theresa mused. Causes give meat to everyday life, but dissatisfaction does not always build into a crusade. Personal disappointments and yearnings have a way of reaching their own limits, like the tension of an over inflated balloon. One last breath causes the explosion.

Theresa realized that she and Kevin were tiptoeing around each other, afraid to cause that last breath. They lived together separately, balancing irritation with the desire for peace. It took energy to argue, and each avoided the confrontation that would lay irreconcilable differences on the table. Each still wanted to protect the other from the pain of separation and the uncertainty of life alone, but what is not acknowledged cannot be changed.

Theresa looked down at the bright red polish on her toenails and rolled back on her heels to wiggle her toes. Kevin would see no sense in painting toenails. She had almost put the polish back on the store shelf when she bought it that week; she'd heard Kevin saying, "Who will see it anyway? It'll just wear off inside your shoes." But she had tightened her grip around the little bottle and said aloud, "But I like it!" An older woman looking at nail files on the same aisle had stopped and stared at her; and then, peering over the top of her glasses, she had said, "Yes, dear, I do, too."

Remembering the woman's deadpan expression, Theresa now laughed as she slipped on her sandals and looked approvingly at her feet. "Score one point for all frivolous expenditures under five dollars!"

She headed back outdoors to move the hose that was watering the lilac bushes. The water trickled across her feet and added more shimmer to the red toes. Gently putting the hose on the last bush, she sighed, "I just like it, Kevin. Some things don't make sense, I guess; they just give silly pleasure."

With ten minutes' soaking time ahead, Theresa went back into the house to change clothes for whale watching. She remembered the advice about the sweater and grabbed a warm hooded sweatshirt. Across the front, it said "Virginia is for Lovers," a wildly successful ad campaign to spark interest in her home state. Her father had considered it a cheap shot, nonsensical and demeaning both to Virginians and to the advertising profession that he loved, but the slogan had caught on like wildfire. It was on bumper stickers and coffee mugs and even on children's pencils and lunch boxes.

Theresa had learned a lot from her father about sales promotion, advertising, and customer feelings. He had had a wonderful way with words and could create a mood or promote a product with perfectly chosen phrases and sounds. "Less is more," he used to tell her. "Know when to say when—say it and leave it." He had always appealed to the best in human nature, believing that advertising had a legitimate purpose in informing about a product or service, not tricking people into foolish decisions. But his style and motives had slowly been pushed aside by an industry in pursuit of big contracts and dollar-driven marketers. For him, advertising had lost its soul, and he himself had become a kind of aging product passing from the scene. With new revelations about her family, Theresa wished she could talk to her father about choices.

Turning off the hose, she called to Gypsy, who clearly looked disappointed at the prospect of going inside. A walk on the beach provided sniffing and adventure, but she trotted obediently onto the porch and lay down.

"Good girl," Theresa said, extending half a dog biscuit as a peace offering. "I'll see you later. Take care of things."

The road to Provincetown was well marked, although the logic of the Cape was confusing. Theresa was traveling north, yet the signs said she was headed to the "Lower Cape." Provincetown sat on the northernmost edge of the Cape on her map, balancing on the fingertips of an arm extending out into the ocean, reaching for the Gulf of Maine. It looked to be the end of the road, the last stop before plunging into water or retracing one's steps. A real outpost, she thought, as she tried to refold the map and slowed the car to observe the passing scenery. Pines thickened, and stretches of sand appeared where grass had struggled or given up. The air was cooler.

Theresa imagined winter here, with harsh, wind-swept days frozen in place for weeks at a time. Tourism and fishing must come to a halt, she figured. What did people do during the dark winter months? Why would anyone choose to live where outdoor life stopped and nature laughed at man's vulnerability? Perhaps the hardy folks of Provincetown curled up like hibernating bears and read books or whittled wood or made babies.

Theresa felt the heat of the sun on her arm as it rested on the open window. The sun's rays tingled her skin, causing the warm sensation to spread, sending sensuous shivers through her whole body. She suddenly wanted to let the sun make her skin hot all over, and she thought of Kevin's touch and the desire she had felt for him in the front seat of her new car. In the early years they had made love often, just for the pleasure of it, and they had conceived a baby—but never seen it. She had miscarried the only opportunity that came. It was a cruel irony that she wrote books for other people's children and would never read them to her own. Their lovemaking had waned with the inability to create a child, causing her whole life to become barren. *She feared the death of desire.*

The narrow road passed through acres of scraggly pines, spaced as if to allow room to grow but stunted for lack of nutrition in their sandy footing. Sun and water were not enough for life to take root in soil that could not sustain it. The sand blew across the road, sometimes blurring the pavement edge and blending into a continuous Sahara. In this desolate landscape, Theresa felt very alone.

A sign pointed to public access of the beach in a state park, and she turned the car toward the parking area. No one else seemed to be around, and she walked the little path to the ocean. Birds chirped wildly in a thicket of low bushes, voicing the urge for mating and spring nest building, thought Theresa. The birds and the bees. She unbuttoned her blouse and let the wind blow through her camisole. It was cool and made her skin feel prickly and taut.

The beach was deserted. A few gawking seagulls paraded along the water, stepping quickly to avoid the creeping tide, poking their beaks into the shallow water for snacks. Theresa marveled at them, at their perseverance, at the repetition in their lives. Why couldn't people be satisfied with that kind of sameness, she wondered; and then she shuddered at the realization that some people could.

She stood staring at the ocean. Not a sign of man or boat. The sun was high in the sky at its noontime peak;

the sand was dry and hot under her bare feet. She lay down on the quiet stretch of beach and bunched the sweatshirt under her head. Her blouse fell open, and she felt enveloped by warmth. The sand cradled her. Theresa slowly pulled her camisole up to feel the sun's warm embrace. She closed her eyes, and her thoughts drifted off to those places of intimacy and passion that stir desire.

The wind blew just over the top of her, not rustling the sand or chilling her exposed body. Asleep or awake were no longer clear in her mind. She felt a hand on the side of her leg, slowly moving across her. The fingers were slightly rough. Soft lips followed, gently kissing her warm body and causing her to reach and yearn for this affection. The hand slid downward, and she felt ready to lose herself in a swirl of attention and need.

The hot sun clouded as a heavy weight came onto her, and she felt legs locking together in rhythmic motion. Her head had slipped off the sweatshirt, and her dark curls pressed into the sand. The two bodies began to roll with the ease of a downhill log, the sun flashing and fading. Sand stuck to glistening skin with each roll, and they held each other with determined purpose and hope. Birds chirped above the sound of moans and waves.

"Hey, lady, are you okay? Lady!" came a voice from somewhere outside herself.

Theresa opened her eyes and realized she was lying at the edge of the water. Her feet were already wet, her red toenails caked with sand. She sat up quickly, pulling down her rumpled camisole to cover herself. Her hair was full of sand, and she was a mess.

"Are you okay?" the voice repeated.

Turning to see the source of the question, she squinted in the sun and saw two men standing behind her, holding hands.

"Oh, yes. I … I'm fine," she stammered, feeling confused and trying to smooth her hair and straighten her clothes. She stood up awkwardly, wondering how she'd gotten so close to the water. Sand fell from her hair onto her shoulders like a shower of brown sugar; her face flushed at the remembrance of her dream.

"I guess I just …" Her body still tingled, and her thought trailed off.

"We were worried about you. From way down the beach we saw you rolling towards the water. When we got close, you didn't move; and the tide is coming in." The man paused, gripping his friend's hand tighter. They were both slim and wore tiny bathing suits and silky shirts. "Not an efficient way to drown yourself."

Theresa couldn't yet see humor in this situation, and she didn't like leaving the unfinished dream. The young man looked relieved that she was not acting drunk or crazy. "And who's Rick? Would you like for us to call him?"

"Rick?" Theresa half whispered, as if saying the name aloud revealed a deep secret. "What do you mean?"

"You kept saying his name. Is that your husband?"

"No, no. I mean … He's not … not exactly … " She felt as though these two strangers had somehow crept into her fantasy, watching her with the faceless lover that she had called Rick. "But thank you for your concern. I'm all right, really I am."

Theresa grabbed her sweatshirt and stumbled up the beach toward the thicket of bushes and the path that would provide refuge from this embarrassment. She didn't look back at the two men still standing at the shoreline. The midday sun was high and piercing. Her body shivered as she got into the car, dropping sand everywhere.

ଔ

Downtown Provincetown felt very different from Chatham. More fish and fewer diamonds, she thought, as she walked the narrow sidewalks lined with souvenir shops and cheap eats. Bars and nightlife beckoned more boldly than in Chatham, and the people out walking seemed younger and less formal. It was a relaxed and tolerant kind of beach town, with lifestyles that shared the sun and the ocean and didn't bother about the differences.

It was easy to find the piers, where fishing boats and whale-watching companies had small booths to sell tickets. Theresa scanned the choices and then walked out to the short line in front of the Dolphin Fleet sign. Ducks waddled among the tourists, as if awaiting their turn for a place on the boat. Children dragged sweaters along the rough planks of the pier, watching seagulls circle above them and reluctantly holding on to their parents' hands.

"One adult ticket, please," she said to the already sun-tanned young woman in the booth.

"For what day?" came the cheerful response.

"For today," she answered.

"I'm afraid this afternoon's trip is already sold out. Could you come back tomorrow? We have space on the morning and the afternoon trips tomorrow."

Theresa thought a moment. She hoped to hear back from Rick and wanted to be available for his call or return visit. Part of her wondered whether it was a good idea to ever see him again, but the rest of her knew she had to see him, to separate out the feelings of dream and reality. *Could she be tempted to have an affair?* She was unsettled in her marriage but had never before been attracted to another man. She felt guilty and eager, curious about the man behind that wonderful grin.

"How about tomorrow afternoon?" came the young voice again. "I recommend the afternoon trips this early in the season; they're warmer."

"I can't tomorrow," Theresa blurted out. "How about the next afternoon?"

"That's fine," was the response. "Please be here thirty minutes before the hour. There's a snack bar onboard. And don't forget your camera; there've been some amazing sightings. The mothers are returning with their calves, and several of our favorites have been spotted."

Theresa wondered how one could have a favorite whale, much less be able to identify an animal so huge as it moved through the ocean. Whales were mammals, she knew, and delivered live babies, but how did they nurse and nurture their young in deep, dark water? *How did a mother feel like a mother under water?*

The requirements of motherhood was not a topic Theresa could ponder for long. She had no experience with it. It was a concept, an idea without form. Her own beginnings of carrying a child had not even reached the point of stirring in her belly, and she was left with just the expectation of it, the empty wondering. After the doctor told them she could not carry a child full term, she and Kevin no longer spoke of it.

She paid for her ticket and turned to look out across the bay. It was a seamless expanse of blue as far as she could see, the ripples so subtle they looked solid enough to walk across. She wanted to step out and begin that walk, the aimless wandering toward the distant horizon. *How did water know where boundaries were? One ocean blended into the next, sea into bay, inlets capturing turns and bends. The tidy divisions man made on land had no relation to the greater, wet areas of his world. Man's efforts to control and make rules seemed puny and comical.* Man is an arrogant beast, thought Theresa, not even mindful of his insignificance.

The sky offered not a cloud to soften the heat of the afternoon, and Theresa felt damp sand still clinging to her scalp, occasionally falling onto her blouse as it dried. One more roll on the beach and she would have soaked her clothes entirely, leaving her cold, wet, and sandy—

instead of just the last. She yearned for a swim, to rinse her body and clear her mind, and wondered whether she could stand the early spring temperature of the water.

She had not gone in beyond her knees at Whimsy Towers and not even worn a proper bathing suit. Several times she had just stepped out of her shorts and waded in her underpants, rationalizing that they looked like a bikini bathing suit bottom anyway. And no one was around to see her slip off her T-shirt as she sunned her bare back lying on a beach towel.

Theresa was not much interested in modesty and couldn't understand why showing one's body was so taboo. Kevin had been startled to see her vacuuming without a stick of clothes, but he soon realized some advantages to the practice. Earlier in their marriage, they had often made love on the dining room floor or against the kitchen counter, sometimes without even bothering to turn off the roaring noise of the machine. Once, during a dinner party with some rather dull guests, they had both glanced at the carpet in front of the sideboard at the same time and burst into laughter. Just an hour before, Kevin had dropped his trousers and lowered his naked housecleaner onto the soft, tightly-woven silk carpet, an antique prayer rug. She smiled at remembering how he could be seduced into non-bedroom lovemaking. And she wondered whether she loved him most when she could break his rules.

Theresa got back in her car and drove a short distance along the road close to the water. She was looking for a place to swim. The first opening she saw was a small space between two commercial buildings at the edge of downtown. Several young mothers with fussy toddlers were carrying pails and baskets and mountains of baby gear; they did not look as though they were enjoying their outing.

Theresa considered for a moment whether she really regretted not being tied to child-rearing for twenty or so years. Children certainly provided instant and specific definition to one's life, precluding the necessity of figuring out some other path. But the loss of time and freedom for the joys of parenthood was a choice not within her control to make. Even a prayer rug and lots of practice could not make it happen.

The traffic thinned, and views of the ocean became more frequent and broad. The wind picked up, and the air was cooler, without the fishy smell that came from the docks in the middle of town. The whale-watching boats were still far out of sight in the ocean, but small fishing vessels and sailboats were close enough to shore to count the number of people on board. Some boats seemed to be at anchor, their fishing poles positioned off the stern; and others trawled slowly, with men in yellow boots ready to haul in the catch. Sails flapped aimlessly on the small sailboats until they got far enough offshore to catch the wind as it billowed northward, and then they lurched forward as if responding to a starting gun in a race.

Water was home to many of these people, Theresa

realized. They knew its moods; they loved it; and some probably spent more time on it than on land. She thought of a heavy wool, cable-knit sweater she had bought in Virginia. The salesperson explained to her that the intricate designs of the various sweaters he sold represented different Irish fishing families, distinctive symbols of their clans and heritage. The small Aran Islands off the west coast of Ireland, where these famous sweaters originated, were a long way from Cape Cod; but she had read that the Portuguese fishermen of the Cape also had unique cable-stitched sweaters, called *torcidos*. When men were lost at sea, their bodies could be identified by these family sweaters when they finally washed ashore. It was a rather grisly prospect and sad to think that some fishermen could not even swim, but stories in the abstract suddenly felt real. Theresa looked out on the scene before her and imagined the fishermen in their warm sweaters as winter winds howled and their boats rocked at the whim of the ocean and its storms.

Her mother had never been found. No sweater had brought an end to her father's and grandmother's anxious hope for her safety or confirmation that hope was lost. They had had to accept loss by default. As time passed, there was no other choice. There was no body to bury, no closure—only stubborn imagining of the horror of her death, alone with the raging sea she could not outwit or outrun. It had snapped her boat and carried her away.

"I miss you, Mom," Theresa said aloud, realizing how odd the word felt on her lips. The imagining of a mother had been in her mind and heart all her life, but coming to the Cape had somehow brought the meaning closer, and she felt the connection to a love and belonging that reached deep inside her. "Dad did a good job," she continued. "You'd have been proud." Tears began to form, and she alternated hands on the steering wheel with wiping her eyes. "He never wanted to be with anyone else. He loved us both so completely, right up to the end."

Theresa slowed the car and let her thoughts drift back to childhood memories of her father and his devotion to raising her. There had been no bitterness or heavy sense of duty, just the acceptance of the path life provided and the joy of following it. "Blossom where you're planted," he'd say to her when she grumbled about classes or situations she didn't want to be in. He had little patience with self-pity. There was no room for regret and no benefit in wallowing. He taught his daughter to stretch and grow and give, without dragging the past along like a dead albatross. "Value the past for what it has taught you," he'd caution, "but don't stifle the present with it or sour the future. Do your best this day."

It was his mantra: do your best. He never condemned her, and she never felt she'd not measured up to his expectations, even with the frustration of algebra and the disaster of violin lessons. Like a careful gardener who watches his plants grow but does not pull them up to check their roots, he cultivated the good in the seed he had sown.

Theresa thought how her father expressed so many of

the qualities often associated with motherhood: tenderness, patience, nurturing, compassion. He was not at all embarrassed to show his feelings of caring and to actively guide his child with gentleness as well as firmness. She wondered whether she and Kevin as parents could have done as well together as her father had done alone. Working out the balance of parenting between two people required sharing responsibilities; her father had had to juggle them all.

Before she and Kevin learned that sexual compatibility did not necessarily produce the outcome of babies, they had assumed that children would come. They had wanted to start a family after he finished law school, and the plan was perfectly laid out, with sensible steps sensibly spaced. The order of it all was a little too precise and predictable for Theresa, however.

On April 1st of the last year in law school, she had leaned over her bowl of fettuccini at dinner and, looking straight into her husband's tired blue eyes, said, "Kevin, I've got some news." He looked up at her, not quite giving his full attention.

"I'm pregnant," she said simply.

The forkful of noodles that was midway to his mouth dropped to the plate, and his arm fell with a thump that tipped the slippery mass onto the table, a rented table of the furniture and life that wasn't their own. "What?" he blurted out incredulously, jumping up and looking to see whether his lap was spattered with pasta.

"How could that be?" he gasped.

"The usual way." She smiled at her confused husband.

"But Theresa, we planned ... We agreed ... I don't have a job or even ..." She could see he was not finding anything good about this surprise. The order of things was disrupted, and he couldn't handle any more stress or a change in their outline for the future.

"Aren't you happy?" she asked, watching him sit down but not touching the mess on the table between them.

"Of course I'm happy. It's just that ..." He was only six weeks from the end of school, and passing the bar loomed large on his immediate agenda. He fell silent with his thoughts.

"Kevin ... honey ... I'm just kidding. April Fool!" She put her hand on his arm as it rested on the edge of the table. "April Fool."

"'April Fool'?" he roared suddenly, like a lion startled awake by a poke in the ribs. "April Fool, indeed! Come here, you rascal!" He grabbed her hand before she could pull it off his arm, and he reached across the spillage to catch her other wrist. Rising and pulling her up out of her chair, he tightened his grip on her and taunted her with a mischievous, "April Fool, April Fool to you!"

His arms locked around her, and she felt his body pressing hard into hers. The taste of garlic passed between them as they kissed, and any interest in pasta was left behind.

"Kevin, we can't," she whispered, her breath quickening. "I'm not prepared."

He didn't stop or even hesitate, as they shifted and

loosened their clothes. He lifted her almost off the ground, her feet barely touching the floor. Reaching both his hands under her, he pulled her firmly up onto him, and she wrapped her legs around his body. The logic of planning and the demands of school melted in the heat of the moment, and Theresa soared in the explosion of closeness with the man she loved. Their careful timetable for family was a distant idea; let the gods decide. Neither could control the urge to tempt fate.

Kevin laughed as they finally caught their breath and began to relax. "Guess this is an April Fool's Day to remember! And happy birthday! I may have given you a long-term gift!" He lowered her to her feet, kissing her forehead.

"You're more of a gambler than I gave you credit for," Theresa replied, straightening her clothes and running her hand through his rumpled hair. She loved the feel of his thick, curly hair and wondered for a moment whether they'd just conceived a child that might have those same curls. But no child came from that day's reckless lovemaking, and as the years rolled along and the timing seemed right, still no child came. A medical diagnosis finally dashed their hopes.

ॐ

Theresa rehearsed the two episodes of intimacy from the past two hours—one in imagination and one from a law school memory in their tiny kitchen. She tried to sort out the details of remembering and assign feelings to both a daydream and a fact of history. She knew that fantasy was the devil of desire, but sometimes the past blurred with wishful thinking. The two incidents began to combine in her thoughts, the rolling, the lifting, the passion, the release. *Could she leave routine for uncertainty?* She knew she loved Kevin the most when he least expected it, when the lawyer was off-guard.

Time and common sense would sort this out, she figured, gripping the wheel with both hands. She hoped that impulse would be tempered by reason and that her instincts would not fly off course for fleeting moments of escape. *Could she have a child with another man?*

Theresa sighed and watched seagulls hover over one of the fishing boats as it approached the harbor. Some squawked mean-sounding alarms of territorial warning, and others followed patiently, almost meekly. They circled and glided, diving occasionally to the water's surface for a quick try at a fish or floating tidbit. The birds established their own pecking order, and the march to the hunt was led by the bold. Theresa wondered whether seagulls dealt with disappointment, whether the stronger helped the weak, and whether birds who could not bear young were left behind.

She suddenly wanted to get back to Chatham. *Was Whimsy Towers home?* Sand cascaded from her hair. The leather car seat felt gritty, as if an hourglass had split open and scattered its measured time. She drove on, blind to the passing dunes and sea grasses, and deaf to the call of the ocean. The siren voice she heard was that of motherhood. She yearned for a child.

Red Rover swallowed up the road as its driver headed south with singular determination. The day's planned outing had been delayed, and Theresa no longer wanted to stop and pass time without purpose. She could have a swim at home. The privacy of her own beach would be a welcome prospect after the real and imagined encounters of the afternoon.

When Theresa reached the house, Gypsy was anxious to be let out, and they walked together across the lawn and down to the beach. As she stepped onto the warm sand, Theresa kicked off her sandals and dropped her sweatshirt. Continuing toward the water, she slipped out of her shorts as she walked, leaving them where they dropped. Next came her T-shirt and then the camisole, each falling to the sand in the short trek to the ocean. Before she reached the water's edge, she stepped out of her panties.

The cool water covered her red toenails and gradually reached her knees, slowly engulfing her with the shock of turning cold. She was exposed and vulnerable, her bare skin feeling the contest of the hot sun against the icy ocean. She dove deeply and then shook her head hard as she surfaced. Sand floated and swirled; her weightless body curled and turned. She wanted both to get out and to go deeper. She wanted to feel warm and safe and yet welcomed the raw chill of being naked and at one with the water. Theresa drifted slowly away from Whimsy

Towers toward her neighbor's empty house. The trail of her abandoned clothes disappeared from sight as she relaxed and let the caressing waves envelop and carry her.

She didn't hear the truck that pulled up next to her house. She was numb and content, watching clouds drift into formations as she kicked and followed their changing shapes. What she did see was her dog racing up the beach, without barking, to meet the visitor in a truck with a shiny hood ornament.

Theresa could see the man stoop to rub Gypsy's neck, and she knew it was Rick. She was relieved it was not the uninvited guest in the boathouse, but she was still far from land and her clothes. He continued to pet and talk to her dog, not looking her way.

After the one-sided conversation she could not hear, she saw Rick stand up and head toward the porch. She could hear him calling, "Theresa! Hello! Anybody here?" He paused to look at the lilac bushes and then knocked on the door, repeating his call louder. She watched him gingerly open the door and go in, wishing she were there to offer him coffee.

When he finally came out, Theresa realized she had no plan. She wanted to call out to him, but she didn't dare call attention to herself.

Rick stood with his hands on hips, looking around. He and Gypsy walked briskly across the lawn, dog legs doing double pace to meet Rick's long stride. As the grass crested above the beach, he stopped, and Theresa could see him looking at the water, searching for her. She knew she just looked like a head with curly brown hair bobbing in the calm water, but she hesitated to acknowledge him. He stood watching for a moment and then waved. She did not respond but began swimming slowly in his direction. He walked toward the water, smiling and waving both his arms. The urge to wade out and meet him was overruled by the obvious dilemma at hand, but he continued towards her. Overhead, a brilliant blue sky with puffs of carefree clouds stretched in all directions.

She saw him look down at her crumpled sweatshirt on the beach. Then he stepped over her T-shirt. Next came the discarded shorts in the sand. He stopped abruptly when the dry sand turned wet from waves and he saw her silky underpants at the edge of the water. She had only a moment to wonder whether he had figured out the situation, for he turned abruptly and headed back to his truck. He didn't stop to pet Gypsy or look back.

CHAPTER NINE

Rick's work boots had left deep imprints in the sand, and Theresa retraced his steps as she emerged from the water, cold, refreshed, excited. He was leaving fingerprints on her life. That night she slept without a nightgown. After the freedom of swimming with no bathing suit, she'd worn only a thin cover-up for the rest of the day, and then slipped naked between the soft sheets. The nights were wonderful at Whimsy Towers—crisp, breezy, and fragrant with a mixture of pine and salt air. A faint hint of blossoms teased its way into the wind, and birds were silent only when the darkness demanded quiet.

She'd gone to bed realizing that another odd incident with Rick was keeping her from calling him about the yard work. She was certain he had been the man standing on the beach, and she wondered why he'd come back to the house. He did not call, and she waited in order to examine her own motives. *Did she want him as a gardener or a lover? She had never had either.*

The phone rang and broke the train of thought that was leading to danger.

"Hello?"

"Hi, Theresa. I've had trouble getting through to you. You must be outside or out exploring a lot."

The familiar voice shattered her reverie and the expectation of someone else.

"Hi, Kevin. Yes ... yes, everything's fine." She'd been rehearsing what she would say if Rick called, and she stumbled to switch gears and realign emotions.

He continued, not delving into her sincerity. "I tried calling all day yesterday, but there was no answer. And last night I had to work late. Hope this isn't too early."

"No, it's fine. We're up. I mean ... Gypsy and I are up."

Her clarification was peculiar, but she didn't dare pursue it. In her heart she had committed adultery, plain and simple. She increasingly thought of Rick and what it would be like to be with him. The rolling daydream from the beach repeated and repeated, but now the man's face was clearly Rick's, and Theresa's imagination carried them to new heights. Her restlessness was protected by distance, but she knew the glue that kept her married to Kevin was losing its grip. Theresa could not quite admit the finality of it, but lack of satisfying companionship makes places empty and uninteresting. She knew she was selfish to think of discarding a good man who wanted her so much, but she did not care. *She was not willing to rot in place.*

Theresa was glad Kevin could not see into her eyes, but she knew he was searching for clues to figure out the moment, to move forward.

She pounced on the lull. "I need to let Gypsy outside. Can you hold a minute, and I'll pick up downstairs?"

Theresa knew he'd be glad for the opportunity to gather his thoughts. *Lawyers liked preparation.*

She grabbed her robe and hurried downstairs with the dog. As she opened the door, her heart pounded, and she froze. Scattered on the porch floor and down the steps were bits of celery, carrots, and crackers. Gypsy scurried over them, anxious to get outside and find a familiar place for her morning business. Theresa slammed the door and turned back to the kitchen. She picked up the phone.

"Kevin, still there? Can I call you right back? I need to do something." She was trying to control the fright in her voice, and she knew she was breathing faster than before. She hoped he'd think she had just run down the stairs or from the back door.

"Is everything okay? You sound a little panicked."

"Everything's fine, but I need to check something. I'll call you back in five minutes. Will you be home?"

"I'll wait right here. Are you sure you're all right?"

She hesitated. "I'll call you right back."

Theresa realized she'd opened up a Pandora's box of choices. Kevin would not be easily brushed off without an explanation of her behavior, and she didn't want to draw him into her web of events. Not yet. *The details of her days were shaping her plans.* She needed more answers herself before she could share her feelings with him—or her decisions about the future. She didn't want to lie to him, but she wasn't ready to tell him the whole truth, either.

Curiosity and foolishness combined as she raced across the lawn to the boathouse. The distance seemed longer than before, perhaps an omen urging her to re-consider. *Should she stop and call the police?* Gypsy caught up with her midway to the pier, and Theresa felt a silly comfort in the dog's company. They had not been back inside the boathouse since that first morning, and she was hell-bent for discovery.

She pushed hard against the door, and it flew open, banging against the wall. It bounced back toward her, and she shoved the splintery boards away again. Hinges creaked. The image of an old Western movie, with the sheriff strutting into the saloon through swinging doors to confront the bad guys, flashed across her mind. She half smiled, but her knees were shaking, her eyes afraid to blink. Gypsy trotted in ahead of her, oblivious to the prospect of trouble.

The room had changed since Theresa first saw it. She stood in the doorway, taking in the whole space, her gaze drawing it together by each corner. Gypsy sniffed and inspected the floor, never missing an opportunity for the quick taste of a wayward crumb.

"Guess our boarder has checked out," Theresa said aloud, the pounding in her chest lessening.

Gypsy's ears perked up, and her tail wagged at the sound of Theresa's voice. The dog seemed reassured by her tone. Tone communicates more than words, Theresa mused, remembering how Kevin's dismissive tone dis-tanced her from pursuing reasonable conversation. Whatever she said to Gypsy, if wrapped in kindness, would be accepted with grateful wagging. Gypsy took her cues from the one who fed her; spouses had more complicated needs. Kevin would not be pleased with her impulsive rush to the boathouse, and he would be right. *Could there possibly be danger in this peaceful place?* Gypsy's tail continued to wag.

The pile of cassette tapes and portable tape recorder were gone. There was no sign of carrots or bags of chips. The bed was made with the tidy precision of camp inspection for the day's clean cabin award. Everything was in order, the four chairs pushed evenly under the table at exact intervals. Theresa didn't know whether she was relieved or disappointed. She stepped into the room, entering the home that had been someone else's. *Who had stayed here? What trespasser would leave with such care?* Her apprehension faded into acceptance and the belief that a friendly visitor had belonged to this room as surely as her grandmother's heart had filled the towers overlooking it.

She left the door open as she called Gypsy and headed back to the house. Her fear of the place was over. Its drafty walls held mysteries that could no longer frighten. It had been cleared of the past, but its ghost still lingered somewhere in the present. She was determined to find her connection to this elusive specter and the reason for corncobs and carrots. New relationships were dawning in her life, leaving gifts at the doorstep of her imagination.

Early morning was cool and damp. The boldness of a golden sunrise crept across the ocean, warming Theresa's back as she followed her shadow across the lawn. The phone was ringing. She ran the last few yards into the house and again breathlessly picked up the receiver.

"Hi Kevin," she blurted. "I'm so sorry. It's just that ... " She stopped to consider where to go next with her explanation. "Kevin?"

There was a silence, and then a voice said hesitantly, "Theresa? ... Hi ... It's Rick."

She closed her eyes, aware that yet another awkwardness had arisen between them.

"Oh! Oh, Rick. I'm so sorry." She realized she was repeating the same words she had thought she'd been saying to Kevin. She started again. "I thought you were ... I mean, my husband just ... " Her thoughts were a jumble.

"I think I've caught you at a bad time. I can call back later, but I felt I owed you an apology from yesterday."

"Oh, no. No apology," she stammered. Theresa forgot all the lines she had rehearsed for this call. Nervously, she added, "Skinny-dipping has its risks." She realized she didn't know whether she meant for her or for him, but he rescued the conversation before she fell deeper into the confusion of her emotions.

"Theresa, would you like to discuss the house maintenance things?"

"Yes ... yes, I would, but now is not a good time. Could you come back to the house?" She decided to keep talking, convincing herself that she could put her thoughts in order and speak coherently. "Is today possible? I'm going whale watching tomorrow."

"Today is fine, if it's around noontime. I've got deliveries scheduled before and after."

"Great, I'll see you in a couple hours. And I promise I'll be dressed."

There was a pause. "Is that supposed to be good news or bad news?" Rick laughed.

Theresa pictured his smile at the other end of the line. He was unaffected and easygoing. She was glad he'd left the beach yesterday before either of them had to decide what to do next. Feeling comfortable around him was one thing, but emerging naked from the water would have sent quite a mixed signal for friendship building.

He let her catch her balance and then asked, "One more thing, Theresa."

"Yes?"

"Do you know a six-letter word that is a 'verbal noun ending in -ing'?"

"What?" she replied, with startled disbelief. "A what?"

"I...N...G," he repeated more slowly. "A verbal noun. I need this six-letter word to open up my crossword. I figured you're a writer and might know. Doesn't ring a bell?"

"Well," she began, "a 'verbal noun.' I...N...G. You mean, like eating or spying?"

"I'm not sure. I guess so. The second-to-last letter is N; I'm pretty sure of that. The cross word is 'purana'."

"'Purana'? What in the world is that?"

"A Hindu epic. Actually, they are a group of legends relating to the gods and creation. It's a fascinating study of ancient fables and lore."

Theresa was dumbfounded. "Rick, what do you teach at the college?"

He laughed. "Do you mean my other talents besides digging perfect holes for lilac bushes?"

She was embarrassed but curious enough not to be put off. "Yes, what else. What lies beneath that easygoing surface?"

Rick paused. "I teach Western Civilization."

"Western Civ!" Theresa exclaimed. "That's a long ride from India!"

"Well, community colleges don't have the luxury of specialization in academic fields. It's pretty much history and Western civ. We're the sampling table for higher education. But my background is in South Asia, and my Ph.D. is in Indic languages."

"Ph.D.! Now I'm really impressed. How did you end up here?"

He didn't immediately answer, and she remembered her hesitancy when he'd inquired about her background.

"I'm sorry. I don't mean to pry," she continued.

"No, it's all right. It's just a rather long story, a complicated story. Maybe sometime."

"How about over lunch? I'd welcome a break from unraveling my own history, and I make a delicious tuna sandwich."

Rick's hesitation was long enough to make her wonder what he was thinking and whether he was still smiling. "I've already packed my lunch for the road today, but I could bring it along to eat at your new table. How would that be?"

"That's a plan," she answered eagerly.

Theresa hung up and almost forgot the morning's alarm over veggie bits and phantom visitors. She was lunching with an interesting man, and the day was ripe for intrigue and excitement. She felt absolutely naughty. Being away from home and from Kevin gave her an imagined freedom that stretched her invisible tether. She wanted to feel free as well as connected, without regret or guilt. It was an improbable combination.

Lack of satisfaction in her life could not be traced to any single problem or omission. It was the accumulation of events, the sameness of action and reaction. The mixture needed a stir, or a new element, but the possibility of explosion bubbled close to the surface.

An ocean breeze crept up the bank and whipped towards the house. The screen door flapped once or twice as the wind changed course and lost its will to enter. Morning settled on the day with both certainty and freshness. A bouquet of fading pink and orange clouds drifted slowly overhead, unobserved, out of reach of the currents below.

The phone rang again.

"Hello?"

"Theresa, what happened? I began to worry when you didn't call back. Then your phone's been busy. Are you okay? You're scaring me."

"Hi, Kevin. Yes, yes, everything's just fine." She searched for an excuse. "I was expecting a delivery and thought I heard them outside. Then they called to set up another time. I'm sorry, the time slipped away." She wondered how convincing she sounded.

"Isn't it a little early for deliveries?"

"No, not really. I guess they need to call early to set the schedule for the day and be sure people are home." She was grasping for credibility.

Kevin didn't ask what delivery she was expecting, and she assumed he chose to let her wiggle in the noose of her own making. There was no such thing as a little lie.

"Theresa, I'd like to come up this weekend. I miss you, and there must be some things I could do to help you around the place. I can fly into Boston and rent a car."

Kevin's way of pursuing a thorny issue was to tack and come around at a different angle. He was a natural strategist, and Theresa felt outmaneuvered. She twirled a lock of hair around and around her finger. Just as she was lining up her troops for battle, the war shifted, and new terrain had to be defended.

"Oh, Kevin, I don't know. I'm still finding my way here, mentally and physically. I don't think I'm ready to open it all up."

"Do you mean open yourself up?"

She hesitated, feeling transparent. "Maybe."

"Theresa, I don't pretend that we can resolve this over the phone, but we need to face some things. I don't want you settling in up there with me in Virginia. I miss my girls."

"Laundry piling up?" she quipped.

She could hear him take a deep breath and knew it was a cheap shot. Kevin did not have a temper, but he often had to calm his anxiety level with her. Conflict resolution required delicacy and patience, and she and Kevin had cultivated them both.

"No, I can handle the laundry. And my shirts don't care who drops them off. But the prospect of a long-distance marriage and being shut out isn't something I bargained for."

Theresa wondered whether her grandmother had heard similar words, perhaps by letter or cable. The written word gave time for reflection before response. Telephones brought immediacy to an issue. She felt the silence hanging between them, waiting for her to step in and chase it away.

"Kevin, having a few weeks apart is not exactly severing our relationship." She stopped, considering the sharp edge of her tongue, and then decided to unsheathe it. "We're able to do that just as well when we're together."

A long, painful quiet engulfed the moment. Theresa realized she had broken the code of propriety; she had dropped the gauntlet, and Kevin was unsure whether to accept the challenge.

"Let's both think about it," was all he said. His instincts as a lawyer fought with his desire to be a good husband. "Let's take the necessary time to consider what we value."

Theresa felt numb and guilty as she hung up the receiver. She was baiting Kevin and had no idea what she expected him to say or do. She couldn't define what she wanted from him or from their marriage. And distance only clouded the issues.

The kitchen was stuffy and smelled faintly of fireplace ashes swept into corners or lodged in the nooks and crannies of the chimney as they rose to the sky. She stood up slowly and walked outside again in her robe, closing her eyes to the morning sun and wondering when rain would come and relieve her of watering the infant lilacs.

CHAPTER TEN

Rick, do you think home is where you're from or where you're going?" Theresa asked abruptly, before he'd even pulled his sandwich out of his lunch pail.

He opened the lid and lifted out several small bags and an apple. She sat patiently perched on the edge of her chair, and he slid his closer to her in order to share the shade of the umbrella. Her face was troubled and intent; her tuna sandwich sat on a bright yellow plate like an unappealing replica of real food. Theresa wasn't thinking about eating.

"I think home is like an anchor," he answered slowly, unwrapping a large sandwich of carefully layered meat and tomato slices.

"How do you mean?"

"Well, I think home is that place deep inside that gives a sense of belonging. It's something we bring, not seek. It's what we develop that nourishes the soul, that includes those we love, even when we're not together."

Theresa wondered whether he was alluding to his former wife. He began to chew, without looking at her. "It's a heavenly place of the heart," he continued.

"So you can throw your heart anchor overboard?" She laughed, hoping to stir him out of wistful thoughts.

"No," he answered quickly. "Remember, an anchor is attached!" His blue eyes sparkled and made the blue of the sky turn pale. "You can lower an anchor into any kind of water, make your home anywhere, and that deep sense of belonging stays with you. It's who you are, not where you're dropped."

"I think we have a runaway metaphor here," Theresa said, feeling a chill at the reference of home and belonging in water. She gazed out at the ocean, thinking of her mother.

"A turtle doesn't have a problem finding his home; he carries it along for all to see," he continued, not put off by Theresa's comment. "We humans aren't usually that clear on what really suits us. We waste a lot of time wishing and hoping for someone else's idea of home to be ours, to fit. It's a disappointing search."

"My father used to say to 'blossom where you're planted,' but I think he always longed for the time he was with my mother."

"Wishing for something out of reach is different from remembering the past with fondness, Theresa. But longing for what cannot be is destructive and hurts those around us as well." He paused and looked at her, setting his sandwich aside. "What happened to their marriage?"

She was still watching the gentle roll of distant waves. The rhythmic motion reminded her of a photograph she had seen inside of being rocked on the porch by her mother. Snuggled and safe in maternal love, she had slept with the certainty of heaven on earth.

"'Heavenly place of the heart.' I like that," she began. "I believe that heaven is a mental concept that we can experience here and now, and our home should definitely be tied to it. Heaven is not a place where we go but an idea, and so is home. They both develop in thought."

Rick did not interrupt her as she pulled these concepts together. Theresa leaned forward, elbows on the table, still focused on the water sparkling with morning brightness.

"She died," she said simply. "My mother died right out there somewhere."

Rick stiffened in his chair, waiting. He did not speak, and Theresa debated whether she should change the subject or continue.

"She was a sailor who loved the sea, and her passion led her into danger that had no mercy. She disappeared in a storm."

"Disappeared?"

"She was never found."

Theresa turned toward Rick, and her eyes were full of tears about to spill. He pulled his chair closer to hers until the white plastic arms nearly locked together. He reached his arm around her, and Theresa leaned into his shoulder.

She sighed as the tears began to drop. "I'm sorry. Being here has been an emotional roller coaster. It's so beautiful and so sad. Whimsy Towers has touched three generations of women in my family."

"And it will touch many more." He gave her a gentle

hug of reassurance.

Fresh tears formed at the unintended reminder that she would not have children to inherit this place. Its history would pass into other hands. The slate would be cleaned of tragedy and joy, and new events and people would begin new history.

"No. No, it can't," she said slowly. "I lost a baby early in pregnancy."

Still staring at the water and struggling to regain her composure, she continued, "My husband's and my blood types have an Rh factor incompatibility. The doctor said I will not likely get pregnant again and could never carry Kevin's child to full term."

"And you believed him?"

Theresa turned to this man she hardly knew who had just challenged the dire prediction that had nearly shattered her life.

"Of course I believed him. He's a doctor; he's supposed to know these things. What do you mean?"

"I just meant that sometimes the fear of a situation takes over and becomes the reality. Bodies can change as our concept of them changes."

"Are you a witch doctor, too, Mr. Ph.D.?"

"No, but I have seen the resignation and downward spiral in people who have unquestioningly accepted some devastating medical news. They lose their fight, their purpose. They become victims in a broad sense, and the joy slips from their lives."

Theresa began to fiddle with the same curl she had

twirled while talking to Kevin.

"Am I to ignore medical science?"

"Not ignore, but don't give in. Don't limit your prospects for a full life. You've just told me how you think of heaven and home. It seems to me that motherhood is also an idea in thought. It cannot be seen with the eyes any more than home can, but it's evident in life through actions."

"It's evident in life through having a baby!" Theresa blurted out. "Having one, not just conceiving one."

Rick sat silent for a moment. "Not necessarily," he began softly.

"Well, I already have a dog. I love her enormously, but it's not quite the same as mothering a child, I imagine."

"No," he said. "Of course, not. But mothering doesn't always mean birthing."

"Do you mean adoption?"

"Why not?" he replied, with the same softness in his voice. "My sister and I were both adopted. Our birth mother was young, unmarried, and unable to stay off drugs. She abandoned us as babies. We know we had different fathers, but there is no record of who they are, or were."

Theresa was jerked from wallowing in her own problems and stared at Rick. He was still seated close to her, his handsome, suntanned features darkened further under the shade of the umbrella. He seemed so steady in his life, so balanced. So at ease.

"Doesn't it make you crazy to want to know who your parents were?"

"It used to, when I was younger. When my sister and I were little, we would dream about running away to find our mother, to convince her to love us, to want us. I suppose we thought we were responsible for her leaving. Children think they are to blame when the bond of love is broken."

"When were you adopted?"

"Evidently quite soon after our mother signed us over to the state. Our parents, the only people we have known as parents, took us even with some residual problems from the drugs passed to our bodies. They always told us we were a special gift to them. It was how they prepared our young minds for the concept of adoption. Their patient love created a healthy family. That's why I believe that motherhood, parenthood, is really about unconditional love and caring, not about who gives birth. We filled a void for them and they for us. They were wonderful parents."

"Did you ever see your birth mother?"

"No. Our parents tried to find her several times. She had traveled west, continuing to seek bad company and a dangerous lifestyle. She died before we were out of grade school. I may even have siblings we'll never know."

Theresa tried to grasp the idea of having brothers or sisters that were unknown, perhaps walking down the street or passing in a store. *A connection that was no connection.* She was an only child because events had dictated it, and her father had chosen to leave it that way. Families were formed intentionally and unintentionally, and the whims of sex did not always seed the best in them. Rick's family had evolved by desire, Theresa's by default. Each had flourished over time from the dedication of parental love. Each was solid and good and left the remembrance of belonging.

"Are your parents still living?" Theresa asked suddenly.

"My mother died a few years ago. My father pretty much crumbled up, and he's now in a nursing home. Mostly TV and crosswords." Rick paused. "That's where I picked up my puzzle addiction." He laughed. "It was something we could do together when I visited him. Now I'm hungry for the harder crosswords, but we still do others together. It's odd the ways we begin to parent our parents."

Theresa noted how his eyes had a faraway look of fondness, and his smile seemed linked to distant thoughts. She dared to continue questioning.

"And when did your first wife pass on?"

Rick bolted upright in his chair. "First wife? I've had only one wife, Theresa."

She wanted to shrink down in her confusion and meddling.

"I thought ... Your ring." She looked at his hands, and he began to turn the ring with his right fingers and thumb.

He replied slowly, looking at the still-shiny wedding

band. "I guess it's part nostalgia and part insecurity. I can't quite let go of her, and I feel safe behind the appearance of commitment."

"Safe from what?"

"Safe from having to go on emotionally, romantically, I suppose. Safe from starting all over in building a relationship."

"Do you mean safe from feeling guilty if you meet someone else?" asked Theresa a little too quickly. She blushed at her impertinence. "I'm sorry. That was not my business."

"No, that's all right. It's a fair question. The initial emptiness after Carol's death has gradually begun to fill with other opportunities to share and be useful. I keep busy with teaching and helping my sister with the business. Remember when I told you that life does move on? I, too, have had to accept that—or prove it. Tragedy can harden us or toughen us; they're not the same."

Theresa repeated the name *Carol* to herself. "How did she die?"

Rick took a deep breath and did not immediately exhale. She could tell he was rehearsing painful events in his head and deciding whether he wanted to let them out. They each had a past that was a graveyard of memories, some good and some not; and he was clearly unable to bury the one of his marriage.

"She was hit by a drunk driver on Christmas Day."

Theresa could not speak. She longed to throw her arms around him and shield him from this hurt. He continued talking, without waiting for a response.

"We were walking to my parents' house, our arms filled with gifts, when a car veered off the road and hit us, dragging her along the sidewalk for half a block. In an instant, my life was carried away in a zigzag trail of ribbons and flying packages. Lying on the ground, I heard screeching and screaming, horrible sounds mixed with the crashing of mailboxes and fences. Everything was turned upside down, a swirl of gasoline and pain and flashing lights. It was over in a minute. When I regained consciousness, they told me she was gone."

Rick leaned back in his chair, taking deep breaths of air as if to fill his soul with new energy. The sun had reached its midday high and cast even shadows on the grass around the umbrella. Huddled together out of the light, they sat in heavy silence.

"I'm so sorry," began Theresa. "How long were you married?" she continued, hoping he'd find comfort in the remembering.

"Just ten months. It was our first Christmas together. We had grown up here on the Cape; our families were neighbors. Carol kissed me when we were seven years old, and that was it. She chased me down the beach until she caught my bathing suit and pushed me down and kissed me." Rick paused and began to laugh. "Pretty aggressive little thing, I guess. I've never even kissed another woman in my life." His eyes danced with the amusement of fond memories, and then he added, "Kissing on the beach in later years became more interesting."

Theresa blushed at the suggestion of intimacy and also because she was wondering what it would be like to kiss him right then and there. She tingled as her daydream of rolling in the sand with him played across her mind. Unconsciously she shook her head, feeling the curls bounce around her ears, and she brushed imaginary sand from her arm.

"Seems like you waited a long time to get married."

"Yes, I had this notion that I should finish my degree before taking on the responsibility of marriage. Carol finished law school, and I finished my dissertation. We needed time apart to focus, and then we got married and decided to take a year off just to spend time together. It was really wonderful. Like two teenagers in love. We had great jobs lined up in Boston for the first of the year, but ..." His voice trailed off. "Without Carol, I decided to stay right here on the Cape. My degree, however, is wasted for any teaching here, and I often feel those school years were wasted, too, since I didn't get other ones to spend with her. But we didn't know. We just couldn't know. And my roots are here."

"I guess that's the answer to my earlier question about how you ended up here. You started here."

"Yes, my reason to leave is what left. My heart is at home in Chatham. My father and sister and her family are close by. It's a great place to live." Then he added, "You should try it."

She searched his face for clues that might add meaning to those four simple words, but she saw only the sincerity of a man content in his surroundings. He was happy, and her heart ached.

"I ... I don't know what lies ahead."

"Theresa, we've covered that ground. Tomorrow is not yours. Only today. What are we each doing with today?"

Rick began to pack up the empty bags from his lunch and took the last sip of his canned lemonade.

"I do know I'd better get back to work today, or my tomorrow will be jammed." He smiled at Theresa as he got up.

"Thanks for coming, Rick. I like talking with you."

"I like it, too, and I didn't mean to unload a lot of old stuff on you. We each have some baggage we're carrying around."

"Yes, we do," said Theresa, smiling back.

They walked together toward the old pickup. Its ram head glistened in the sun, pointing to the ocean. Silent seagulls rode gentle blue crests, pecking at the water and occasionally flapping their wings for balance. The air was still. A persistent ringing of the telephone from inside the house met only deafness.

CHAPTER ELEVEN

Sharp barking startled Theresa awake, and she bolted out of bed, trying to focus and figure out the cause of Gypsy's commotion. The dog was moving from window to window, tail wagging and then stopping, lifting herself to the level of each sill but unable to be satisfied with what she saw or couldn't see.

Suddenly the sound of a small engine or motor filled the morning air, bursting in on the grogginess of sleep and confusion. Something was definitely going on outside, and it was close to the house. Gypsy became more agitated, barking louder to challenge the sound below.

Theresa hurried to the closest window, still without curtains, and leaned out. As she stretched further to see around the corner, leaning as far as her tiptoes would allow, she steadied herself with outstretched arms, and her nightgown slipped loosely off her shoulder. Gypsy nuzzled her, as if asking to be told what was happening. Theresa looked down at the dog and then back to the yard as a riding mower came into view, with Rick at the wheel.

This time he didn't look away when he caught her by surprise. She pulled back, clutching at her gown, not completely covering her body and not caring. She noticed how brown her skin looked in contrast to the pale pink fabric. Theresa felt desire, mixed with remembering. Rick waved sheepishly and headed the mower in a straight line toward the water, away from the house.

"It's okay, Gypsy; it's Rick."

She pulled on a sun top and wrapped a bright floral skirt around her, tying a knot at the waist. Hurrying barefoot down the stairs, she fluffed her hair with her hands. "He's come to tame the jungle grasses." She laughed reassuringly to both the dog and herself. But she knew she felt like a hungry native girl in the jungle, anxious for the work of the day to be over and the pleasure of the night to begin. She wanted to be close to this man, and she didn't care about the rules of the game.

As she pushed open the screen door and started down the steps, a folded piece of paper caught her eye. It was stuck in the first lilac bush, close to the ground. In bold printed letters, it said simply, "Feed Bobby O.K.?" No signature, no addressee. The list of names, men's names, associated in some way with Whimsy Towers was growing longer: Claude, Stormy, Bobby. *Was there any connection between them? And why was permission needed to feed Bobby? Or was Theresa being asked to feed the mysterious Bobby?*

The momentary distraction of the note was forgotten as she saw the riding mower swing a broad turn and head in her direction. Rick was smiling and waving, and she ran to meet him.

He throttled down the powerful mower. "Good morning! Thought I'd get an early start before we have to call in some goats to get this grass down."

Theresa heard the words, but she just stared at him and watched his eyes meet hers, hoping for what she felt when he saw her in the open window.

"I guess we still never got to the business of your taking care of things here."

"No, I guess not, not officially. I just came on the assumption that we'd work it out. I pretty much know what needs doing, unless the lady of the manor has other ideas."

He smiled that broad grin that found its way to her heart and caused her common sense to disconnect from reason. Theresa couldn't tell whether his comment was searching for cues from her or was an honest request for gardening input. She walked slowly around the humming mower, watching him watching her. Like a calculating feline assesses her prey, she circled him with anticipation. He was too good and too kind to approach a married woman, even a vulnerable one. It was she who chose to attack.

"How about a ride on your chariot?" she asked, putting a bare foot next to his leg and beginning to climb up.

"These things aren't exactly made for two," he said, offering no resistance.

She sat awkwardly on his lap, with one arm around his neck, and he enclosed her with both his arms on the wheel.

"Ready? Hold on." The mower jerked forward, and Theresa settled more firmly against the worn softness of

Rick's blue jeans and flannel shirt. Her face was close to his, and the earthy smell of cut grass began to mix with the scent of her night lotion and bath powder. His arms were strong and firm around her, occasionally holding her a little tighter than the jostling of the mower seemed to require.

They cut a dozen or so rows before Theresa let her face touch his, her hair tickling his neck. She lightly kissed his cheek and felt him lessen the pressure on the gas pedal. He turned to her, his eyes full of questions, and they kissed with the ease of two people who knew they should.

The mower veered off to the side, destroying the established pattern, but the kiss lingered, and the previously charted course was changed.

"Theresa, I don't know that this is a good idea," Rick whispered, but held her tighter. "I ... I don't think we should be doing this."

The mower was carrying them along like a runaway stallion, and Theresa was not getting off. She felt his body contradicting his words, and she turned around to straddle him face on. The mower came to an abrupt stop. Her legs wrapped around him in the seat, knees pointing to the playful clouds above, and they kissed again, and again, without objection. Rick pulled her toward him, his hands reaching under the wraparound skirt, and he soon found she wore nothing under it. Her skin was smooth and warm. He struggled to reach the zipper on his jeans, and she lifted herself up and helped him unzip the path of no return.

They had not heard the blackbirds in the tall oak near the house. The birds were screaming with alarm and anger, but no warning was loud enough to slow the racing speed of passion. As if on signal, dozens of birds flapped noisily out of the tree, leaving the branches bare and quiet. But stillness couldn't mask the face of regret.

"I've dreamed of this," said Theresa breathlessly, not caring that the steering wheel was pushing into her back. "And it was wonderful."

"Theresa, I ... I don't know what to say. We had no business ... "

"I know. I know you're right," she said, pulling herself up from him and straightening her skirt. "I know it was wrong, but I'm not sorry. It felt so right and so special."

"And so selfish on my part." Rick was trying to put himself back together. "I haven't been attracted to any woman since Carol. You've caught me off guard, Theresa from Virginia. And I feel guilty as hell."

"Because now you've kissed another woman?"

He looked at her with a quizzical smile. "A little more than a kiss, wouldn't you say?"

She blushed and pushed back his hair with both her hands. She sat content.

"Theresa, you are a married woman. I don't want to mess with that. You're very attractive and desirable, but that's a game I don't want to play."

Theresa felt like a sixteen-year-old caught in the backseat with someone else's boyfriend; it was she who had really transgressed. She had done worse than step outside a trusting relationship; she had smashed the barrier of the forbidden and let animal instincts run wild. She had committed adultery without dreams and imagining, and she loved it and wanted more.

"We need to promise not to do this again," Rick continued, as if trying to convince himself, but he still cradled her on his lap, kissing the curls pressed into his face.

"I can't promise," she said simply.

"I can't be dishonest, Theresa. I can't pretend this is real … or right."

"Can I blame it on the seductive rocking of the mower? 'The mower made me do it'?" she teased.

"No, the desire of the moment made us both do it. We felt close and at home with each other. So natural and so ready. Theresa, we are both hungry for love, but an affair is not going to satisfy either of us." He smiled at her with enormous tenderness. "At least not for long."

"It's the guilty conscience thing," she said quietly, as if she was being scolded.

"Of course it is. That's why we care for each other, feel comfortable together. We value goodness and the desire to do what's right. We want to love, but we fell off the track, and it's wrong for both of us."

She could not argue with him, although her heart called out that she wanted to change her life and live for the moment, climbing forbidden peaks and not caring about the consequences. She felt warm and safe in Rick's arms. Perhaps the future was not theirs, and they had only today, but it had been sweet.

A mist hovered on the ocean as the sun blazed through the morning haze, reaching higher and higher, casting a wild prism of color across the water. The sun rose each day without invitation. It struggled to brighten the sky no matter what obstacles Mother Nature threw in its path. Dust or clouds and rain could veil the power, but the source of brightness didn't change. It could be hidden but not cancelled. Its strength had no lasting opponent.

"Rick, are you happy?" Theresa asked, watching the water change into soft rainbow hues melting across the surface as the mist tried to lift.

Still holding her warm and comfortable on his lap, he answered, "Are you referring to the extraordinary last few minutes of my life or a broader time frame?"

She poked him and stared straight into his eyes. She wanted to understand her feelings and have a glimpse into a heart that was whole, even with its shadows of the past. She trusted him and felt a closeness that she craved. The discontent in her marriage was wrapped in a web of confusion, and Theresa wondered whether it was to be endured or confronted. Being satisfied with one's life was the challenge of the ages, and she yearned to know the recipe for healing.

"Gratitude," he continued. "Forget the 'be happy' business and focus on gratitude. You'll find that 'happy' is what you bring and not what you get. Waiting for something good or better or different is what keeps half of humanity in a state of limbo and empty expectation. Large doses of gratitude create happiness."

"Is this the old 'glass half empty, half full' query of life?"

"You bet. And the glass is definitely half full ... and filling. Forget empty; it's the road to misery, and you know about misery's desire for company!" Rick laughed and tried to shift Theresa's weight on his lap. "It's a mighty big pit to fall into, complete with a welcome mat!"

"And what's the other half of humanity doing?" she continued. "The half not waiting around for happiness to land on them?"

Rick became serious. "They don't have much time to wonder if they are happy, or even should be. Their days are consumed with the necessities of existence, the most basic demands. Clean water, enough food, keeping their children safe and healthy. They don't have the luxury of whining." He paused, and Theresa saw that faraway look return to his face, a look of fond remembering, tinged with resignation. "Injustice sings out from the soul through random placement of birth. One day in India would graphically show you what I mean."

"India! I've never even been outside of Virginia, that I can remember, before last week. I'm afraid my grasp of the world is pretty much academic." Realizing she would not be able to corner him on the ways of the heart, she pursued his comment. "And when were you in India?"

"Graduate school. I lived there for a time and then

made several other trips to complete my research. Carol used to say that if I hadn't fallen in love with her first, she'd have worried about the competition from my distant muse."

Theresa thought of the dining room table inside with the inscription about muses. She wondered for a moment if muses could be male as well as female. Jealousy was an odd companion, and she had often entertained it herself while Kevin was in law school. He spent long hours with fellow students in the library and in study groups. She wasn't certain whether she was unhappy with the school, with him, or the people who claimed his time, but she had been alone and outside the circle of activity. Late-night calls for Kevin were often from women, and she could hear him talking in low tones from his desk in their bedroom. But Kevin was too conscientious, too honest, and probably too exhausted to be tempted by any woman on the prowl, student or not, and Theresa's anxiety dissolved at graduation.

His law office was a mistress she could handle, and the results of the relationship benefited them both. He moved quickly through the ranks of approval and accomplishment, carving a niche among the partners with his diligence and competence. He was excited, focused, and their life began to build with the certainty of success and contentment.

And then the easy conversation and sharing began to fade. They each were wooed by the subtle temptress of overwork, the pull of self-importance. Silence filled the spaces of their time together. There was less affection, less touching, less caring, and Theresa knew before she acknowledged it that her marriage was slipping to that place where no one would come looking for it.

"Did Carol practice law?" she asked Rick, who was contentedly watching the gentle rhythm of the ocean.

"No, she never had the chance. She passed the bar on the first go and her job in Boston was waiting for her, but January never came. It's a cruel loss of talent."

Then, shifting his weight and pulling her close to him, he whispered in her ear, "Don't you think it's a little odd to be talking about Carol just now? I have to sort through that on my own."

Theresa kissed him, feeling desire and intrigue. They were parked in the middle of a half-mowed lawn, and she didn't care who might see them. Pulling her skirt up over her hips, she felt the hot sun on skin usually out of view.

"I care about you, Rick, and I'm curious about the women in your life."

"It's a short list, remember?" he said. Theresa wanted to slip off her skirt and lie with him in the grass. "My mother, my sister, and Carol. Each with a slightly different role, I'm happy to say. But each with a profound influence on me. You'll be interested to know that my favorite professors in college were often women, and one of the most renowned scholars of Indic languages is a woman."

"What did you give her for Christmas?"

"Dr. Sentasse?"

"No, silly. Carol."

"Now why in the world would you want to know that?"

"It was your first married Christmas together. What did you give her? Is it too intimate?"

Rick sat perfectly still. Theresa was trying to figure out this puzzle of a man and was asking him to return to a painful day in his life.

"I gave her a fuzzy yellow sweater and a plate," he replied slowly.

"A plate?"

"It was a Christmas plate, like a platter. In the center was an elegantly dressed reindeer cavorting in the rain with boots and an umbrella. Across the top it said 'Vixen' and underneath, 'You are the sweetest rain, dear.'"

Theresa said nothing, just watching him remembering.

"She had made Christmas cookies and was carrying the platter of frosted and sparkly cookies to my parents' when we were hit. She died in the sweater I had given her just hours before. It was so soft and ... so soft ... " His words couldn't give shape to his agony, and Theresa joined in the silent sorrow of missing a loved one.

"The platter was shattered, and the cookies scattered, of course. Our damaged packages were retrieved from the scene, but the bits of 'Vixen' were everywhere. For weeks and months I would spot a shiny piece under a shrub or washed to the curb. The cookies were a gift to the birds, manna from ashes, but the plate chips did not go away, like the grief that won't give up."

"I love rain," said Theresa softly, with no apparent reason.

"So did Carol," came the quick response. "She loved the sound, the smell, the cleansing freshness. She used to say that a gentle rain was sweeter than candy and healthier for the disposition."

"I think I would have liked her."

"I believe you would have liked each other a lot. Two kindred spirits, both a little unpredictable and pushy."

"Pushy!" exclaimed Theresa, trying to stand up from her tangled position and poking at the crumpled flannel shirt. "Pushy? You think I'm pushy?"

She laughed as he tried to grab her hands, and they almost fell off the mower as he kissed her to stop the taunting.

"From what you've said about your grandmother, you seem to be her cookie cutter duplicate—sugar and fire, no ice."

She looked at him carefully for signs of disapproval, but there was none.

"My husband might disagree with the ice part," Theresa mused aloud, realizing she had not thought once of Kevin while making love with Rick. It was a cold woman who felt no guilt.

"I wish I could know more about my grandmother," she said.

"Why not go talk with her nurse?" answered Rick, matter-of-factly.

CHAPTER TWELVE

Theresa fumbled through the pages of the telephone book to find the library number but soon gave up and called the operator. Even if it meant missing her afternoon whale-watching trip, she was determined to find her grandmother's nurse and talk with her. She had assumed the woman had moved away and did not even think to ask the bank trustee. Impatience was catching up with her.

"Hello? This is Theresa Crandall calling, and I'm looking for a woman there who knew my grandmother, Theodosia Hampton."

There was silence on the phone line, and she thought she might have been disconnected. She wished Rick had remembered the woman's name. He had met her only one time before she moved out of Whimsy Towers. She had showed him some things around the house and where supplies were kept. It was weeks later that he recognized her at the library desk, and he'd just smiled and waved.

Suddenly a voice said, "Ana's off for a few days. Could I take a message for her?"

"Ana?" Theresa said half aloud and half to herself, remembering the woman watching her with her grandmother's seashell. "Could I have her home number?"

"No, I'm sorry. I'm not allowed to give that out. But I'd be happy to give her a message."

Theresa began to bite her fingernail, a nervous habit she had not done in years. She wanted to jump through the phone and yell at the faceless voice, "But it's important that I talk to this woman. I need to talk to her!"

She calmed her impatience and didn't want to speak until she could trust herself to be civil.

The voice spoke again. "Would you like for me to take a message, to give her your number?"

"Thank you. Yes. Yes, I would."

Theresa gave the number and reluctantly turned to get ready for whale watching. She looked at her fingernails and thought perhaps some nail polish would keep her from biting them. She had time now to think of her morning with Rick, but painted fingernails would not stop her growing confusion or the changes that were happening.

She felt reluctant to bathe. Water, sometimes the symbol of life and continuity, also had the ability to erase, and she wanted to hold on to this last hour and its wonder. Theresa felt alive. She dropped her wrinkled clothes on the floor. A quick shower, she realized, couldn't remove the feelings, the longing, the satisfaction of being with Rick. The connection was more than physical, but believing she could not become pregnant left her free to savor the forbidden thrill and its future possibilities.

Gypsy sat watching her brush her hair with hard, decisive strokes, each pull causing the curls to spring out and then settle softly around her face. The dog seemed to sense that preparation was underway for something, and she stayed close to Theresa in order not to miss whatever was about to happen.

The "Virginia is for Lovers" sweatshirt lay tossed in the corner of the bedroom, untouched since the beach episode in Provincetown. Sand still stuck to it, and Theresa decided not to disturb the crumpled bundle or stir her recollections of that day. The dream was over; reality had overtaken imagining.

She grabbed a reversible slicker and headed downstairs, with Gypsy close on her heels. In the dining room she stopped abruptly and read the inscription on the marble again: "TABLE OF THE MUSES." She, too, was feeling pulled by distant voices—the temptation of adultery, the mystery of Bobby, the hope of meeting Ana, the secret of a seashell. She wanted to draw this strange chorus closer and hear what they had to say to her.

Reaching down, she picked up a shopping bag that sat next to the window and walked purposefully toward the back door. Heavy contents shifted in the bag.

"Hold down the fort," she called to the dog, leaving her for the first time without a pat.

The drive to Provincetown felt somewhat familiar, and Theresa laughed when she passed the park entrance where she had encountered the two men. They had been startled by a woman rolling toward the surf, and, in retrospect, she was startled at the sight of two men holding hands. She hoped their paths would not cross again.

Surely there were enough new roads to follow in life without retracing the embarrassing ones.

Hurrying down the long pier, she saw warmly dressed adults and kids in T-shirts already boarding the boat for the afternoon trip. Theresa wondered why children often seemed so oblivious to temperature, either not noticing or not caring that cool weather required more clothes. One girl wore a bright yellow shirt with detailed pictures of a dozen whale tails on the front; each looked different and had a name under it. Theresa remembered holding Gypsy as a puppy and playing with her, looking into her eyes and deciding what to name her. How does one name a whale, she wondered.

"Hi, welcome aboard. Tickets, please. Thank you." A young woman with the most amazing hair stood at the edge of the pier and helped everyone with the last step onto the boat. Her waist-length strawberry hair billowed out in the wind like unraveling strands of gold streaked with sunshine. She was suntanned and fit, with an easy smile and watchful eye. "Mind your step. Yes, there are restrooms inside. Tickets, please. We'll be leaving in just a few minutes."

"Is there any particularly good place onboard?" Theresa asked as she handed over her ticket, clutching her shopping bag.

"You'll probably want to move around when we get out a ways, but I'd avoid the bow for awhile if you don't want to get sprayed. It feels great on a hot afternoon, but I don't think you'd like it much today."

"Thanks," she replied, grateful she'd brought the slicker, and automatically following the aroma of brewing coffee. Minutes later she was seated on a sturdy wooden bench with a plump young family from Pennsylvania. With the bag tucked securely between her feet, she sat happily drinking coffee and eating a hot dog covered with chili.

"Ever been on a whale watch?" the woman asked her.

"No," replied Theresa. "This is my first time. How about you?"

"Well, my husband and I came here on our honeymoon eight years ago and went out. We haven't been back to Provincetown since. You know … uh … because of the couples thing here. We just weren't used to it. But the kids are so excited about seeing whales, and we can't afford to travel to the West Coast or Hawaii. They're little enough to concentrate on seeing the whales and not take in the rest of it."

Theresa was curious but decided not to ask about "the rest of it." She was enjoying the gentle roll of the boat, still docked at the busy pier, and the warm afternoon sky filled with seagull squawks and the fishy smell of the ocean. She glanced down protectively at the bag at her feet, the bag that held her father's ashes. This was the day that would fulfill his wish to be scattered in the ocean. By joining her parents together, Theresa would be finally separating herself from them both. She was anxious to be underway, and too much conversation with strangers might lead to questions she didn't want to pursue.

As if responding to a silent prompt, the woman asked, "What's in your bag? Brought your lunch?"

"No, it's just something I brought from home."

"Carrying around your valuables here?" The woman's hearty laugh caused her layered chins to jiggle. "Shouldn't bring things on a boat that might fall overboard," she continued, still staring at the bag. "Except for children, of course." She laughed a bouncy kind of laugh that caused her whole upper body to shake.

Theresa was grateful that the bench was bolted to the floor. She wanted to get up and move away, but she realized she would be with these people, trapped on a boat, for the next several hours. There would be no escaping.

She had brought her father's ashes in hopes of slipping them privately overboard. It was not a place for ceremony, she realized, as she looked around at the motley crowd, chewing gum and jockeying for positions at the rail. She stared at the faces and wondered about the lives, the marriages, the disappointments of these people. And she decided she didn't want to say goodbye to her father in the company of strangers.

"We're ready to go," a voice boomed through a loudspeaker. "We expect calm to moderate sea conditions today. Please note that smoking is not allowed inside or on the lower deck. Also, the Coast Guard requires life jackets be available for each ..." A sudden loud screech ended the announcements, and Theresa felt grateful for the return to nature's sounds of seagulls and water lapping the side of the boat. The sun felt warm.

Then engines began to stir, and the smell of diesel fuel blanketed the scene. As heavy lines were lifted from the pilings, the boat slowly, and noisily, inched its way out into the harbor. Children scurried from side to side, searching the water for signs of fish and throwing bits of crackers and hot dog buns to the circling gulls. Anticipation was building for the adventure ahead.

"Hi, I'm back," said the same voice from the earlier blasting. Theresa looked up and saw the young woman who had taken the tickets. Her hair was loosely braided and twisted on top of her head; she held a megaphone.

"Now we're in business." She sighed and laughed. "And now we're ready to talk about whales. My name is Hannah, and I'll be the naturalist on board today to talk to you about whales and their environment. The biggest problem facing whales is man. Fishing lines, propellers, illegal hunting in some countries, accidents, and foolishness take huge tolls on whales. We need greater care in protecting them." She paused, as if debating whether to pursue this topic or go on. "I hope we'll see some humpback whales today. Their calves are really playful, but the adults are not very fast, so first I want to tell you how they get their food."

She held up something brown that looked like a section of coconut frond. "This is baleen," she explained. "It's from the mouth of a whale and is used like a strainer or screen. The whale opens his mouth and lunges into a school of fish, squeezing the water out while holding onto the mass of fish in his strainer. It's a lot of work, but a whale can expand the capacity of its mouth like an accordion. I hope we'll see some whales feeding today. And I'll give you a hint—keep an eye out for bubbles."

Theresa's eyes scanned the open water ahead. The air began to cool as the boat left the harbor. She felt a sudden apprehension at heading out into the ocean. Her heart pounded. A mixture of fear and dread gripped her. Passing over the hidden depths of these waters made her throat catch, and she couldn't swallow the coffee in her mouth.

She began to gasp and choke, her free hand reaching out frantically for support. The remainder of her coffee spilled over her legs, and the cup fell to the floor. Nearby passengers rushed to help her, but she ran past them to the boat's railing and let her insides go. It was humiliating.

Someone handed her napkins, but she continued to lean over the edge, trying to regain strength in her knees and not wanting to face the curious onlookers. A man came next to her and put a steadying arm around her waist.

"You okay?" he asked.

She felt foolish and lightheaded, with only the strong desire to be invisible.

"Do you feel better?" he continued. His voice had a Southern accent that ate the "r" off the end of his sentence.

"Better than what?" she stammered, then realized how unkind she sounded.

"Better than cheap chocolate on a first date."

"Than what?" she asked, slowly turning her head, wanting to laugh but not quite able.

"Cheap chocolate on a first date. It's just a saying. Cheap chocolate doesn't make much of an impression."

"I'm not exactly in a position to comment about making an impression." Theresa laughed, wiping her face with the napkins. "But thank you for your concern."

He was still holding onto her, and she made no effort to move away.

"Would you like to sit down?" he asked.

Theresa nodded, and as she turned to sit on the closest bench, Hannah arrived with a damp towel.

"Feeling better?"

Theresa smiled and glanced at the man with his arm through hers.

"Better than cheap chocolate on a first date," she replied.

"Than what?" asked Hannah, looking first at Theresa and then at the man seated next to her.

"I'm fine, really. I just had a sudden fear or something. I feel all right now. Honest."

"You might want to go on the upper level for some fresh air," suggested Hannah. "It's a little breezier, but it's farther from the engine, and the sun is wonderful."

"Thanks, I believe I will."

Theresa stood up, testing her sea legs.

"Okay if I come with you?" asked her new guardian, also standing.

"Sure, if you'd like to," she answered, not certain whether she cared either way.

The man motioned to two little girls who waited nearby. They had on long pants and matching red sweaters appliqued with turtles. The littler one had buttoned her sweater by skipping a hole or two, and it bunched up across her stomach, causing the turtles to look as though they were climbing on each other.

"My name's Jeff, and these are my daughters, Katie and Elizabeth."

"Hi, girls," said Theresa, heading for the stairs to the upper deck. "I'm Theresa."

"How do you do, ma'am," came the reply, almost in unison.

Theresa stopped and turned back, bending down to turtle level. "Where are you girls from? Where do you live?"

"South Carolina, ma'am," answered the girl with the correctly buttoned sweater. "We're on vacation to see a whale. Daddy says that whales are gentle, and they don't eat people. But Elizabeth wants to go inside a whale, like Jonah."

"Oh, Elizabeth, I don't think that's a good idea," said Theresa, instinctively rebuttoning the little girl's sweater. "Whales have their own special place, and we're here just to watch them."

She was beginning to imagine writing a book about two young sisters and their trip to visit a whale. She wished she had her notebook and sketchpad with her.

"But Miss Bessie said!" cried out the younger child. "She said that Nathan was swallowed up by drink. 'He was in the belly of trouble, but safe with the Lord.' He had to stay in that belly 'til he went holiness. 'Big as a whale,' she said, 'that's about the size of the trouble.'"

"Elizabeth, I don't think this lady wants to hear about Miss Bessie and Nathan," said Jeff kindly.

Properly buttoned, the child stood silent.

"Oh, sure I do. I'd love to hear more. Who is Miss Bessie?"

Elizabeth looked tentatively at her father. "She takes care of Katie and me when Daddy goes to work and Mommy can't ..." She stopped. "When Mommy can't get up or ..." She stopped again, and tears began to fill her eyes. "She makes cookies with us. Her face is black, and her apron has a big pocket."

"Who is Nathan?" asked Theresa gently.

"Nathan is Miss Bessie's brother," interrupted Katie. "He's tall as a giant and gets into trouble. Once the police came to our house looking for him. Now he's stopped drinking, but Mommy can't stop."

Katie looked down at the floor, her eyes showing wisdom beyond her years. "I love Mommy," she said.

"We all love Mommy," Jeff echoed softly. "And Mommy loves you girls more than anything in the world."

Theresa looked around, wondering whether the mother was on the boat, perhaps slipping Scotch into a soft drink at the concession stand or throwing down a cold beer while the family helped a sick lady in distress. She knew little about alcoholism, but she did know from recent experience that you couldn't turn your back on temptation. If not challenged, it will win.

She crouched down and smiled at the two little girls, so savvy yet innocent. She put her arms around them, hugging their red turtle sweaters and pulling them to her heart.

"I bet your mommy is very proud of you," she said, feeling the longing of a parent's love.

And then she suddenly bolted upright and ran towards the bench where she had sat with her coffee and hot dog. The family from Pennsylvania was gone—and so was her shopping bag.

Theresa felt sick all over again, but in a way that drained only her color and left her standing wide-eyed and helpless. She didn't know where to go. The keeper of the ashes had let her guard down and carelessly abandoned her father's trust.

"Seals!" she heard someone scream. "Look! Seals!"

Passengers hurried to the side of the boat, huddling together to catch a glimpse.

Hannah's voice came over the megaphone. "There are harbor seals on the right side. Starboard, for you boaters. These seals usually head to Maine for the summer, but a few will stay at the Cape."

Theresa's eyes searched the moving crowd for the missing family or her white shopping bag. She began to stare at everyone's hands to see what they were holding or carrying. Binoculars, pocketbooks, extra sweaters, lunches. She raced toward the rail, frantically looking for the familiar round faces from Pennsylvania. Enveloped by eager tourists, she stumbled along and again leaned over the edge. Nausea had given way to panic. An elongated reflection of her head bounced on the waves alongside the boat.

Focusing on the outline of the harbor as they picked up speed in open water, she watched the disappearing scene. She was headed for a trip with no purpose. She didn't want to see whales or think about life where she knew there was death.

The buildings and trees of Provincetown were fast becoming distant miniatures, left in the wake of the noisy boat. There was no return and no exit. Shades of blue began to overlap in the water and sky, and excited voices danced in the wind. Theresa needed the air of the upper deck. She needed space, and she was determined to find the energy to search every inch of every level.

Heading quickly to the metal stairs, she spotted a woman with a small child dragging a large white paper bag. With the frenzy of a wild cat attacking its prey, she ran towards the woman and lunged at the little girl, grabbing the bag as the child screamed.

"Help! Help! Mommy! Help!"

The terrified woman turned to see a desperate and tearful Theresa sprawled out in disarray. Next to her was the ripped paper bag, with a satiny blanket and large brown teddy bear tossed to the side. The little girl was struggling to pick up her bear.

"Oh, Teddy! You hurt my Teddy!" the child cried, lifting the stuffed animal that was half as big as she was. "You hurt Teddy!"

"I'm so sorry. I'm sorry," Theresa sobbed, burying her head in her hands. "I've lost my father." Another crowd began to form.

The protective mother scooped up her child and said angrily, "Are you crazy? I doubt your father would fit in a carry bag! What's the matter with you?"

"No, I mean … He's dead."

"Lady, you should stay home to work out your problems. Don't go around frightening young children with your grief!"

Theresa wiped her eyes but made no effort to get up. "I'm so sorry. I just thought … The bag …"

Her voice tried to continue, but the now-turned heads didn't care to listen. Woman and child hurried away as Hannah appeared through the staring faces.

"What's going on? Is everything okay?"

"That seems to be the question of the day for me," Theresa replied, trying to regain her composure. "I've lost something very valuable."

"What is it?" inquired Hannah. "I can make an announcement over the speaker."

Theresa hesitated. "It's a … It's a white shopping bag."

"A shopping bag? What's in it?"

Theresa looked around at the gathering eyes, wishing a huge whale would surface and flip them all into the ocean.

"A box. Just a kinda heavy box."

"Okay," Hannah said. "I'll check around, too, but please let's try to handle this without inciting a riot." She shook her head and laughed. "I don't want to have a burial at sea for misbehavior!"

Theresa shuddered. Still sitting on the deck floor, unable or unwilling to move, she saw two red sweaters with colorful turtles approaching through the towering onlookers.

"Come on, Theresa, we'll help you up."

The two pint-sized girls took her hands and tried to steady her as she got up. Jeff was right behind them and once again put his arm around her.

"This is becoming a little embarrassing," she said, but feeling grateful for her second rescue.

"It's okay. I'm sorry to admit that Katie and Elizabeth are old hands at distress. They've seen their mom in situations where she couldn't get up at all. Just totally passed out. What happened here?"

Theresa was on her feet and realizing that Jeff was directing her to the stairs, away from the gawkers and up toward the open air. They sat down on a bench slightly protected from the wind, looking like a family snuggled close together.

"I've made rather a mess of things," Theresa began, fighting back tears and feeling irresponsible, without answers. She was not used to loss of control.

"Can you tell me? I'm a good listener. Are you alone

on the boat? Should we get anyone?" Jeff asked.

"No, no. That's part of the problem." She took a deep breath and was glad to see Katie and Elizabeth turned toward each other playing a game with long black string twisted around their fingers. She continued, "When my father died, it was his wish that I scatter his ashes in the ocean, where my mother had died. I brought the ashes on this boat, and now they are missing. Right after I boarded, I knew it was not a good idea. Too many eyes, too little opportunity. And now somebody's picked up the bag; it's gone."

As she finished her sentence, Hannah's voice came over the megaphone from the lower level, asking whether anyone had seen a white shopping bag.

"See," said Jeff, "it will turn up. You'll see. Try to enjoy the trip."

They stood and walked in silence on the open deck. The wind blew their clothes and hair, but the sun was warm and welcoming. Jeff directed his daughters' attention to dolphins that followed close to the front of the boat, riding the bow wake. Their sleek shiny bodies leaped completely out of the water, diving down again with Olympic precision, splashing and twisting through the waves.

The girls giggled and pointed. Theresa felt the bond between these children and their father, and she remembered her own father's patient love. Parenting is forever, she thought, as she realized how much she still felt her father's influence. He would always be part of her.

"Bubbles right!" came Hannah's excited voice through the megaphone. "At about two o'clock. See the bubbles? Keep watching. Keep watching! Whales will soon come up to the surface."

From the upper deck the view was fabulous. It was easy to see a growing darkness just beneath the water not far from the boat. Bubbles erupted over a broad area, and seagulls hovered anxiously.

"Keep watching," Hannah repeated. "Whales blow bubbles under a school of fish to trap them."

The boat's engines idled down, allowing it to roll with the gentle current. Passengers scurried for a better view, and Theresa found herself caught up in the excitement.

Sighs of disbelief and wonder filled the air as two enormous whales came to the surface and then curved slowly back downward, their tails slicing through the water.

"Wow!" hollered Jeff, with unabashed enthusiasm. "Did you girls see that?"

He was talking to Theresa as well, and she stooped down to pick up Elizabeth.

"Can you see okay, Elizabeth?" she asked, holding her tight.

"You can call me Liz," the little face replied.

Seconds later the whales showed themselves again. And again. Everyone was squealing with disbelief at the size of the animals and their closeness to the boat. Hannah continued to share information while all eyes onboard were riveted on the churning water.

"These are humpbacks, and they have very few external differences. Markings on their tails allow us to identify different animals, and we take lots of photographs to keep a good record. Some we have seen over and over for years. They bring their calves back, too, and we watch them grow and return. The migration of humpback whales is strongly determined by the females. They seem to like to return to what they know. Any women on board feel that way?" She laughed and paused, letting the drama have its own moment.

Hannah's words were an informative backdrop to the incredible scene taking place. One of the whales rolled slowly over onto its back, sliding under the water and flapping its fins as if clapping for attention. It seemed not at all bothered by the presence of the boat. The day was beautiful, and these gentle-looking mammals were enjoying the luxurious freedom of their own vast environment. As Theresa saw the large eyes peer out of the water, she wondered whether the whales were fascinated by people-viewing. Their needs were food and safety from man—probably not much room for curiosity.

"These waters are rich in zooplankton for the whales to feed," continued Hannah. "Part of what we study is the density of food to support various species of marine life. Coastal ecosystems are very fragile, and we're always on the lookout for changes made by man that will affect the future. Do you kids know what 'endangered' means?"

She waited a moment and then explained the threat of extinction for various forms of life on land and sea—only several hundred right whales remaining in the entire North Atlantic, diminishing numbers of humpback whales, the damaged nesting areas of the roseate tern in the Cape.

Theresa felt her world expanding. She stood holding a small child with comfort and ease, laughing and sharing. She felt part of a family that was not hers. She thought back of being with Rick in the morning and held Elizabeth closer. She felt needed.

The next few hours passed easily with Jeff and the girls. They moved about the boat, watching whales breach in the distance or dive in unison, the patterned and irregular flukes leaving a clear signature on the way down to feed. Several dozen whales made an appearance for the appreciative crowd. Sometimes seagulls rode the noses of relaxing whales on the surface, like sentinels standing watch on an aircraft carrier. One calf rolled playfully around in a pack of seaweed, close to the mother who was probably still nursing it.

But everywhere Theresa went she kept her eye open for signs of her shopping bag. When she finally saw the family from Pennsylvania, she asked them about the bag. The parents said they had not seen what happened to it; the children did not look at her. She pressed them but to no avail.

The wind died down as the boat headed back into the harbor at Provincetown. Across the speaker came an eerie sound of deep muffled, elongated squeals, a rhythmic pattern with rising and falling intensity. Hannah explained that this was "the song of humpbacks," an actual recording of their sounds. "Sung only by males, the sounds are subject to many interpretations, whether for navigation, for mating, or other possible reasons. There are still many mysteries involving whales because they are so difficult to study in their live habitat."

Theresa listened to the mournful sounds and wanted to cry. She could not help but wonder if her father's ashes had already joined the whales in the mystery of the deep.

"Could you watch the girls a minute while I hit the men's room?" Jeff asked. "I can stand outside while they go together into the women's, but I don't like to leave them alone when I go."

"Of course," said Theresa, already holding their hands as they watched the town come into focus.

Minutes later a smiling Jeff emerged carrying a crumpled white bag.

"Theresa! Look what I found in the stall!"

She turned and gasped at the sight. He walked toward her cradling the squished bag like a baby.

"I ... I think you might want me to hold onto this for a bit," he said gingerly.

"What do you mean?"

"Well, um, somebody's broken into the box."

Theresa's face turned white, and she gripped the girls' hands so tightly Elizabeth cried out. Jeff made no effort to hand over his package.

"How about I see if I can get another container or bag and tidy this up? Are you okay to stay with the girls a minute?"

"Yes, of course," she said, feeling her knees want to give out from under her. "Let's just sit a second, okay?"

The silent trio sat down, and Jeff hurried off to the concession stand to search for a new bag. The boat was almost ready to dock when he returned carrying a cardboard box that said, "brewed fresh, tastes best." It was all he could find.

"Listen, Theresa," he began, "I asked Hannah if there are ways to put ashes to rest in the ocean, and she gave me a great suggestion. Interested?"

Theresa nodded, ready to be guided out of the predicament she had created. She felt foolish that she'd thought a public excursion would provide the right opportunity for a private moment.

"There's a fisherman in town who takes people out who want to scatter their loved ones' ashes. He does this mostly at night but sometimes in the day if the fishing's not good. Called 'Van Storm Charter Excursions.' Want to check it out while we're here?"

Theresa nodded again, partly in agreement with the answer Jeff had found and partly in recognition that the time was really at hand to say goodbye to her father.

Engines revved as the double-decker boat nudged its way back into the slip midway on the long pier. Squawking seagulls paraded up and down the weathered planks, heads bobbing, eager for treats or the arrival of a fishing boat with serious scraps. Theresa took a deep breath, still clutching little hands. The gulls scattered, making way, as the pretend family stepped onto the pier and began their search for Van Storm. *Days at the Cape didn't seem to end the way the mornings outlined them. Expectations fell off course.*

Charters were returning with their smiling, sun-burned customers, and it was easy to find Van Storm on the adjacent pier. He had just come in from the day's fishing and was washing down his small boat. Theresa was surprised to see that he was quite an elderly man, trim and suntanned, steady on his feet as the boat rocked with the harbor current. A cap pulled down tight covered his hair, but his eyes sparkled with a blue twinkle.

"Mr. Van Storm?" she inquired.

He stopped and stood up, turning with a slightly amused look.

"I guess so." He laughed. "But mostly I'm called 'Stormy,' unless you're with the IRS or something. How can I help you?"

Theresa stared at the man, looking at his easy smile and friendly eyes. The tip of a tattoo was visible just beneath his rolled-up sleeve. His arms were muscular, his hands coarse from labor on the sea. But his manner was gentle and kind.

"Did you know my grandmother, Theodosia Hampton?"

Jeff looked at her incredulously and was the first to answer. "What? What are you talking about, Theresa?"

The old man's eyes widened and filled with tears. He looked up at Theresa standing on the pier with a fondness that seemed to still all the movement around them. Even the seagulls hushed.

"I've held you in my hands," he said slowly, lifting his upturned palms toward her as if offering an invisible gift. "You're Theresa, Emily's beautiful baby. I've held you and fed you. I watched you crawl and take your first step." He paused. "Oh yes, I knew your grandmother. She was my heart, closer to me than my breath. Warmer than the sun itself."

He rolled up his sleeve and showed the tattoo, a perfectly shaped heart with a tower inside.

"I can still see her standin' on that balcony, watching, waiting. She'd wave her arms so hard I feared she'd fling herself clear off. She was my Penelope, and I loved her from the day we met. Comin' home to her was what made going to sea so sweet."

Jeff stood in patient silence, waiting for a clue to what was going on.

"How did you find me?" Stormy asked, bringing the mood back to the present.

"The shell, Grandmother's seashell. I found it in her safe deposit box with your note. We came looking for you for help in scattering ashes, and then you said your name was Stormy. It just hit me somehow. It just popped out."

He closed his eyes and smiled the most loving smile of remembering Theresa had ever seen. He was alone with a memory, happy and wistful.

Suddenly he opened his eyes. "Whose ashes?"

"My father's," she replied, motioning to the box Jeff was holding. "He asked to be returned to Cape Cod, to be reunited with Mother, with Emily—in the ocean. This is my friend Jeff and his daughters, Katie and Elizabeth. We just met on the whale watch, and they've really been helping me."

"Well, how about we all go out right now," suggested Stormy. "The law requires we get out a ways."

Theresa was too overwhelmed with the events of the day, and she needed to get home to let Gypsy out. She wanted time to think things through.

"Or how about tomorrow?" he continued. "Sunset is a beautiful time. Peaceful and quiet."

"That sounds perfect," she said. "Jeff, will you come back?"

Jeff was listening intently and watching this odd reunion. "I'd be glad to come, but I don't think it's the best activity for the girls. I could get a sitter and maybe take you out for dinner first."

Theresa looked at Stormy, and he nodded agreement. She instinctively jumped down onto his boat and hugged him. The fishy smell of the ocean filled her lungs—and it was good.

CHAPTER THIRTEEN

Tell me about the name 'Theodosia,'" Jeff said as soon as they were seated at the restaurant the next day. Theresa reached for a warm roll. It had sprinkles of vegetables and tomato bits in it and was so soft her fingers left deep prints just picking it up. She held it under her nose, inhaling the yeasty aroma.

"Did you ever bake cookies or bread with your mother or grandmother, Jeff?"

"Not really. I do remember going to Grandma's at holidays and loving to be in her kitchen. My mom wasn't much of a cook. Her job had long hours, and she didn't have time to stir things up in the kitchen. Cooking was work, not pleasure."

"Stormy obviously loved my grandmother a great deal. And my mother, Emily, was so loved by my father that he never considered another woman. But I have no memories of either woman. My dad did his best at the mom activities. We made cookies that you slice off as you squeeze them out of a refrigerated tube—no measuring, no experimenting, no mistakes. Rolling out dough and feeling flour between my fingers came later from my own desires as a homemaker." Theresa took a bite of the soft roll.

"Was your grandmother from the South?"

"What a funny question. Why do you ask?"

"Theodosia is a famous name in South Carolina. The-odosia Burr Alston was the daughter of Aaron Burr, vice-president of the United States, and was married to Governor Joseph Alston in the early 1800s. They owned a large rice plantation in the Lowcountry, along the coast, but she is remembered primarily because of trage-dy."

Theresa looked up with full attention; her middle name was Alston. "Just old Southern connections," her father had once said. "A family thing." She kept her maiden name when she married Kevin, not because of family history but because it was the identity she was used to. She didn't want to be repainted with an unfamil-iar brush.

"What do you mean, 'tragedy'? What happened?"

"Well, she was the daughter of a controversial politi-cal figure, raised in New York, talented, well-educated. She had excellent prospects for a young woman in socie-ty. Then this dashing and wealthy young man from South Carolina crosses her path after spending time at Princeton. Her father was a huge influence in her life, and he encouraged the match.

"I guess it took some smooth talking to woo her to the South and its slower pace, but she finally accepted, and they were married at the turn of the century."

Theresa listened to the events of happiness that were leading to tragedy, and she felt the parallels building from her own family history.

"A baby boy was soon born to them, and they moved into the Alston family plantation, called The Oaks, when Joseph could legally accept his inheritance—at age twenty-four, I think. Although Theodosia adored her child, her health was not good, and she was depressed and frail from the demands of her new life. The long, hot summers in South Carolina were particularly unpleasant because of the fear of what was called swamp fever. Affluent planters usually left the lowlands during the hot months and retreated to other homes inland or in the mountains to escape what we would probably call malaria. Often the slaves were left in charge of the rice plantations.

"The Alstons spent summers at their property inland, except one year when Theodosia and their son accompanied Joseph for political campaigning. They briefly returned to The Oaks and the surrounding area, where their son was evidently bitten by an infectious mosquito. He died that summer at age ten.

"The parents, of course, were devastated. Their only child and heir."

Theresa sat spellbound, totally uninterested in the crab cake dinner that cooled in front of her. "What a horrible shock. Their future snapped off like a twig."

"There's more," continued Jeff. "Distressed and seeing no hope for the future, Theodosia wanted to go back to New York to see her father. Aaron Burr had been vindicated from shooting Alexander Hamilton in a duel and later found innocent of treason. He'd had his own series of problems and had gone abroad for awhile. Now his daughter hoped that a visit to her father would give them each needed strength. She wanted Joseph to go with her, but the nation was at war with England; and he was, after all, governor of the state."

"Oh, no!" Theresa interrupted. "What happened to her?"

Jeff took a deep breath. "She drowned. Her ship was lost at sea in a terrible storm off the coast."

"Oh, no, no … No!" Theresa put her head in her hands. She leaned forward with her elbows heavy on the table, steadying the slow shaking of her head.

"Theresa, I'm so sorry." Jeff leaned across the table, reaching out a hand to her shoulder. "I didn't mean to upset you. What is it?"

She took a deep breath and slowly lowered her hands to her lap. "Maybe it's a Theodosia curse, a black cloud. It's the battle of happiness struggling against the overwhelming odds of defeat. It's my naïve wish for a happy ending to every story. Hollywood can wave a wand, but the rest of us have to accept the roles we're given." She paused. "What did Joseph Alston do?"

"He basically became undone. He felt alone, severely ill, uninterested in politics and life. His world had fallen apart, accompanied by floundering rice markets and increasing debts. He and Aaron Burr continued to hope for a miracle, that Theodosia would be found, but he died a broken man several years after his wife.

"Strange tales have passed through the years of a disoriented woman who looked like her wandering to shore and people who swear they saw her or her ghost, but Theodosia's fame is mostly preserved through the facts of her tragic story. I had never heard of anyone else having that name until you mentioned your grandmother. You're not going to tell me that she, too, drowned?"

"No, but she did come from South Carolina. She was raised there, married there, and then seems to have run off to Cape Cod to escape an unhappy marriage. She was drowning in life, not death. Her only child was my mother. When I was not quite two, my mother died in her small sailboat in a sudden storm off Chatham. Mother lost her life, and Grandmother gradually lost her mind. I guess my father didn't have the option of crumbling; he had me to look after. My full name is Theresa Alston Crandall."

Jeff took in the far-reaching effect of his story. "I'm sorry. I should never have told you all that stuff; I had no idea."

"No, it's all right. I'm really glad to know the history. It's fascinating." She sat thoughtfully for a moment and then asked, "How do you know all that, anyhow?"

"I guess I'm kind of a history buff. I've visited all the Civil War sites in our state and studied a lot of the local history. We are often accused of not catching up to modern times, of living in the past with Confederate flags and rebel yells, but we're not all barefoot and bitter, lamenting the outcome of 'the years of unpleasantness.'"

"'The years of unpleasantness'?"

"Yeah." He smiled. "That's what some folks call the Civil War or 'the War of Northern Aggression.'"

"I guess our viewpoint does color history." Theresa laughed, tasting a bite of delicious chunk crab. She liked this man, with his Southern drawl that stretched vowels out into separate syllables. He was attentive and caring. He'd had to assume a similar role to her father's, but his wife was physically present while he took over responsibility for the children. A woman with children who could not be a mother, and Theresa was a woman without children who wanted to be a mother. The irony of life twisted her heart.

"Think we better get going soon?" Jeff asked, finishing the last prawn from his seafood platter. The discarded tails were lined up in a perfect row. Kevin would do that, thought Theresa, and then realized she hadn't thought of Kevin or called him that day.

"Mind if I make a quick call?" she asked, rising from her seat.

She found a pay phone and tried a collect call. There was no answer.

"I'm ready if you are," she said to Jeff as she returned and reached down to pick up a box from under the table. "I'm ready for another parting at sea, and I think I'm doing okay with it."

Stormy was waiting for them on his boat. The teak trim looked particularly shiny, and chrome strips caught the fading sunlight. There were cushions on the wooden storage benches, and all fishing gear had been cleared off.

Small colorful flags on the lines flapped in the harbor breeze, and what looked like red bandanas were tied at intervals along the metal guidelines. There was something clean and festive about the old boat. It looked higher in the water than the day before, as if lifted above the current, reaching upward.

Stormy was dressed in corduroy trousers with nap so new it looked as though he'd not yet sat in them. He wore a warm navy turtleneck sweater that matched his navy knit cap. His weathered hands were scrubbed and steady as he helped Theresa and Jeff onboard. She smelled a hint of spice as she passed him and sat down on one of the cushions. She wanted to ask whether her grandmother had ever been on this boat, but she tried to focus her thoughts back to her father and the business at hand. Theodosia could wait another day.

"Thank you for doing this with us, Stormy," she said. "You've really saved the day, and with such a meaningful connection. You, of course, knew my father."

"Yes, I was around him for several years, and I liked him a lot. He was a very devoted man, Theresa. Thoughtful. Fun. Crazy about your mother and you. We had wonderful times together at the house. You were the center of attention after you were born, and we all felt we'd gone through that pregnancy together!" He laughed, and the wrinkled lines in his face deepened with the joy of remembering.

"We watched Emily's belly grow, and I recall the day your father told her she shouldn't disappear alone down the beach anymore. She didn't much like being told what to do, but she didn't offer a peep of resistance to the idea. I think she knew it made sense. It was too cold to go sailing, but she loved to walk the beach. Your dad didn't want her givin' birth in a sand dune someplace. She was an independent thing, that Em, just like her mama."

Theresa had a million questions to ask about her mother and grandmother, and here was a man who had the answers, but this special evening was for remembering her father. She wanted to fulfill his wishes with love and gratitude for his devotion to her. He had been her whole family until Kevin, and the voices now creeping from the past would have their own time to be heard.

"Ready to cast off?"

Stormy was already loosening the lines from the pilings. Theresa nodded and held her box tight. It felt heavy on her lap. She was holding her father in a way she had never imagined, and they were traveling together at last to meet her mother.

Jeff sat close to her. He did not offer to hold the box or to help Stormy but sat quietly, allowing them each to reflect on the situation that brought them together. Theresa briefly wondered whether Jeff was taking time away to sort through issues of his marriage as well. *Did men think about their marriages—or only about their wives?*

Early evening was a quiet time on the water. Tourists had already left the piers to find dinner or other amusement. Fishermen had returned with their catches, washing and readying their boats for the next day's departure.

Nets dried in graceful folds, like shawls draped across a chair after the party. Stars began to appear above the ghostly gray horizon, and bits of somber orange flickered through the darkening trees from a distant sunset behind Provincetown.

Theresa thought for a moment how much cheerier this boat trip would have been in early morning. She daily marveled at the huge, fiery ball that slowly pushed up to the glistening wet surface, revealing itself only in small amounts, teasing the viewer with its majesty. She watched with wonder this special gift of coastal living. Brilliant layers of gold and yellow shattered like fairy dust across the sparkling water as the sunrise took over each day. And then quiet ripples carried the color away.

Stormy was the first to break the silence. "Life preservers are in the benches under you. Anybody feel the need to put one on?"

The two passengers shook their heads, and Theresa realized that Stormy might be trying to gauge her fear as well as being obedient to Coast Guard regulations. Unconsciously, she patted the side of the box on her lap.

"We'll go a little further out than required," Stormy continued. "I thought you'd like to be clear of the night fishers and anchored parties. This is a private time, and I want you to feel private. It's a beautiful night, warmer than we've had."

Theresa turned her face toward the bow and let the wind blow her hair straight back. She was beginning to like being on boats and the feel of the water passing along under her. She closed her eyes and tried to imagine sailing, without the noise of an engine. Sailing must create an incredible closeness to the water, she thought. A closeness and trust.

About twenty minutes passed without further conversation. The gray sky blackened, blurring the line between water and heavens. Scattered stars reached down around them, and a bright moon held its place, not quite full or perhaps no longer full. Theresa was better at observing sunrises.

Stormy slowed the boat and removed his cap. "How about here? The wind is calm, and the ocean is ours. Does it feel okay?"

Theresa wasn't sure what would ever make this business feel okay, but she sensed that of all the choices she could think of, this was going to be the one.

"Yes … yes, it's fine. Thank you, Stormy. And thanks for decorating your boat for us. I'm just so grateful we ran into you."

She knew that tears were about to come and that they were for meeting this man who was so close to her family, as well as for saying goodbye to her father.

"Love takes shape in many ways," she said softly to herself.

Stormy shut off the engines altogether, letting the small boat drift and bob. The lights on the boat seemed to twinkle, challenging the stars, and the red bandanas fluttered on the lines like butterflies trying to catch their balance. He let his passengers get used to the calm and the feel of being rocked by a great and gentle hand.

"Would you like to say a few words, Theresa?" Jeff asked.

Theresa wiped her eyes and hugged the cardboard box. "Daddy, I love you. Thank you for a beautiful life. Thank you for always being there for me, for loving me even when I probably didn't deserve it. Thank you for your wonderful sense of humor, your patience, and your orange pancakes." She laughed through her tears. "We had a lot of fun, and you will always be close to me. I miss you, Dad."

A muted sound of bells began to echo across the water. Theresa turned and saw Stormy holding a long rack of brass bells wrapped with colorful bits of cloth. He shook them slightly, and joyous, tinkling sounds of celebration filled the air, dancing with the moonbeams.

"I got these when I was in the Pacific years ago. They've sent many a cold ash into this ocean, but the hearts always linger with the living. They stay with us always, Theresa."

She smiled at this wise and curious old man. For a few minutes the bells rang, and grief was postponed.

"Guess we better do what we came for," Stormy said. "You come around on this side, so you're workin' down wind. Not much blowin' tonight, but we don't want any surprises. Your dad wouldn't want to be flyin' around aimless-like, makin' a mess. It wasn't his nature!"

He laughed softly and held onto Theresa to steady her at the railing. She carefully opened the box and leaned out over the dark water, so black and cold-looking she wondered how life could stand to be in there.

The box was awkward in her arms, and Jeff helped her tip the open end toward the water. The first ashes swirled high in the air and blew far out across the surface, landing beyond their view. Together they shook the box lower, and the remainder of the ashes floated like delicate snow, fine and fluffy, before settling on the water. Some blew on wind rows with the current, then slowly sank into the blackness.

Theresa stood watching with the empty box, wondering how the accumulation of so much lightness could have been so heavy. She whispered, "Goodbye," but knew that the letting go was not over.

"Godspeed, my friend," Stormy said with such tenderness that Theresa turned to look at him. The tips of his fingers brushed his forehead in a simple salute, and his watery eyes reflected the lights of the boat and the sorrow of many goodbyes. He reached down and picked up a long, curved piece of wood with intricate carvings and thumped it with a padded stick.

The haunting, mellow sound of the gong repeated again and again. Tied butterflies struggled to get loose, and a watchful moon stood guard.

CHAPTER FOURTEEN

Theresa was anxious to get back to Whimsy Towers. The hour-long drive gave her time to think about her life, the thirty-four-year prologue to this trip, and the visible and invisible imprints she'd left in getting here. The future sometimes raises its curtain slowly. She sensed that happiness and fulfillment depended on the improvement of moments, the gradual realization of promise. *Had she wasted the years? Could she figure out the direction forward for her life?*

The lights she'd left on inside gave the house a warm glow, with moonlight spreading over the roof. She stopped the car midway in the drive. Tomorrow she had plans to see Stormy again, and he would tell her things about this place that would bring the past right to her door. Whimsy Towers would no longer be a painted lady with secrets; she was about to be exposed.

Theresa heard Gypsy barking as she pulled up and turned off Red Rover. Hurrying around the corner of the house, she wondered what the commotion was about. Gypsy was standing inside the door, barking anxiously, while wagging her tail with enthusiastic greeting. The front of her was on guard-dog alert, and the back half was pet-me friendly. Protective, eager love was a great companion, thought Theresa, as she glanced around to see whether anything looked amiss. Gypsy stopped barking only when Theresa let her race outside, eagerly sniffing the porch floor and following a scent that hung in the evening air.

"What's the matter, girl?" asked Theresa. "Everything's okay." She tried to reassure her furry detective, but then her eyes fell on a folded piece of paper tucked under one of the large flower pots. There was not enough light to read the note, and her heart pounded with apprehension as she went inside. The phone began to ring.

"Hello, Theresa? It's Jeff."

"Well, hi."

"I just wanted to be sure you got home all right and were doing okay."

She didn't remember giving Jeff her phone number.

"Oh, yes, I'm fine. And thanks again for all your support. You've been my guardian angel, being there when I needed help. You really were the one who brought this all together, and it was a beautiful evening."

"I was an unknowing facilitator!" Jeff laughed and then became serious. "I enjoyed being with you and meeting Stormy. He seems like quite a guy."

"Yes, I look forward to getting to know him. He's a gift of new family."

The phone line became quiet, and then Jeff said, "I think relationships have a way of replenishing themselves. The players change, but the relationship connections get refilled. Do you think that's a cold-hearted way to think of it?"

"No, I suppose that's a very practical way, a healing way. People do not stay in our lives forever, but fresh beginnings have risk—and disappointment." And then she added, wistfully, "I think what we hold onto is safety, wanting the certainty of the familiar, but I wish I could talk with my father and ask him why he kept Stormy and Grandmother a secret."

Theresa could hear the waves through the still-open door. Crickets offered their night song, and Gypsy had disappeared into voiceless prowling. The lullaby of wind, water, and darkness was pulling her drifting thought away from conversation. She yearned to sink into the deep cushions and dream of birthday cakes and lacey socks, hamsters wearing pink bows, and Easter eggs hiding in the bushes. She wanted all her yesterdays. She wanted to line up the people from her life and be reintroduced.

"Theresa, are you there? Hello?"

The voice startled her, and she remembered with a jolt that Jeff was still on the phone.

"Oh, I'm sorry. I was just thinking .... "

"That's okay. I know you've had quite a day, and I won't keep you. But, Theresa ... " He hesitated. "Could I see you again?"

She tried to focus her drifting mood and understand what he was asking. The silence lingered a little too long.

"Maybe you could join the girls and me for a picnic," he began. "Or a beach walk. We're experts at finding sea treasures. Have you seen the gorgeous colored pebbles on the beach? They're like rainbows just under the water. Provincetown is full of surprises."

Theresa laughed to herself and wondered what Jeff really meant.

"That would be fine," she replied. "You have two very nice little girls, Jeff, and I'd like to see them again."

She suddenly realized it sounded as though she wanted only to see the children, but she lacked the energy to retract her words or fumble through innuendo. Let it be. After all, she was not positioning herself for a relationship, and friends set limits by behavior as well as words.

"They liked you, too, and that sounds great! I'll call you in a day or so."

Theresa was touched by his enthusiasm and genuinely grateful for the help he had been to her, but she was tired, exhausted beyond civility, and feeling adrift in new currents. She briefly closed her eyes. Oddly, she wanted to call Kevin.

Leaning back into the pillows of the couch, she gazed at the kitchen ceiling and saw the painted life preserver ring with the words, "Too Late." She said Kevin's name aloud and reached to dial the number, but the room closed in and gently carried her off with the painted angels, slipping between the clouds.

She awoke in an hour, still clutching the recent delivery. Slowly unfolding the paper, she saw the same careful handwriting as before. Theresa needed answers about these nibbles and notes! She paused as curiosity chased dread, and then began to read:

I run fast when the ocean calls. Trees hurry by the other way as we pass. They sing in wind of danger and sorrow. They echo the whisper of lost baby. I look for her. Every day I look for her. The water is empty of babies, but the clouds look down with softness. Tree voices tell clouds to make a pillow for the baby. She can trade her cold wet sleep for softness. I look for her. Every day I look for her.

Theresa read the note several times and felt strangely comforted by it. The writer of these words was not a threat to her or a danger. *A poetic and thoughtful stalker?* This writer had an aching soul and a desire to help. There was love in these words. *But who was the lost baby? And why was the message at Whimsy Towers?*

She reached again for the phone and dialed Kevin. A groggy voice answered on the third ring.

"Oh, Kevin, I'm sorry. I didn't realize it was so late. What time is it?"

"Are you calling to set your clocks?"

"No, Kevin," she answered, not sure whether he was being humorous or irritated. "I wanted to tell you about my day."

"At midnight? Is everything okay?"

She seemed to be asked that question rather often recently. She put it aside for future thought and did not answer.

"I buried my dad tonight. And I met Stormy. He took us out this evening in his fishing boat."

She did not explain the "us," but let it float in the space

between them as if she meant her father. Theresa had not talked to Kevin since before the whale watching trip and losing the ashes the day before, and she had news to share that was safe and nonthreatening to their marriage. Her clipped sentences did not immediately convey the information or betray her emotions. She could tell that Kevin was waiting patiently for the details to unfold.

"It was really peaceful. The ashes just melted into the water. A painless union."

She was rehearsing the evening as if talking to herself.

"Nobody else was anywhere near. Just us and the vastness of forever water and sky. Mission accomplished. My parents are together again."

Her midnight musings were eating up her husband's scarce sleep time, but Theresa needed to sort slowly through the events that were opening up Whimsy Towers, and Kevin was part of the discovery process. She wanted to include him, but only from a distance that would allow facts without personal exposure.

"How did you meet Stormy?"

"That's a miracle!" exclaimed Theresa, eager to share her new connection to the past. "I went on a whale watch, and someone there recommended him as a way to send off ashes to the sea. When I met him, I asked if he knew my grandmother. I mean, how many 'Stormys' can there be? What do you think the odds were of that happening?"

"Just enough. Besides, I thought you didn't believe in chance."

"No, I don't really. I believe that things happen with purpose, that there is a plan. I don't think I was there by coincidence."

"Where does he live?" continued Kevin, which avoided a philosophical detour.

"I really don't know. We met in Provincetown. He has a small fishing boat, and I assume he's a fisherman and takes out charters. I have so many questions! I'm going to meet him there tomorrow for dinner—or rather, tonight, I guess. Want to be jealous of a weathery old man?"

She hadn't mentioned the other two men she had spent time with, and she suddenly blushed with the memory of Rick. Kevin didn't pick up the bait, and she was glad not to go down that slippery road. She wanted Kevin to know what she was discovering about her family but not about herself.

"I'll be anxious to hear what you learn," he said.

Kevin's response was his way of wrapping up the conversation. Useful information that would open closed doors of the past was coming in installments. Theresa knew that until she had peace of mind, they would both be unsettled by her restlessness.

She fell asleep on the couch, stretched out full length on the flowery cushions. Still warmly dressed from being out on the water, she dreamed of walking the beach, looking for a lost baby, calling helplessly in the wind. She walked and walked, as if the beach had no end and the search had no answer.

A faint scratching sound startled her, and she opened

her eyes unwillingly. A little more time. She needed a little more time to find the baby. Feeling exhausted from the dream, Theresa lay still and watched the clouds float on the ceiling. Daylight filled the room. She felt the soft cushions around her and realized she was in her own house, and there was no baby.

The scratching persisted. Theresa sat up and heard short bursts of whimpering from the direction of the porch, a mournful plea of distress and expectation.

"Oh, Gypsy!" she exclaimed. "Oh, Gypsy, girl! I forgot you!"

The dog had spent her first night outdoors. Theresa saw a rounded indentation in the fresh mulch around the lilacs, just about the size of a middle-aged, curled-up Labrador.

"Thanks for staying close to home. Let's have some breakfast," she said as she followed Gypsy into the kitchen and began to turn off the lights. "It's going to be an exciting day."

Gypsy munched her dry food eagerly, as if hungry for the return of familiar routine. The tea kettle whistled a piercing, loud scream as the phone rang. Theresa ran for one and then the other.

"Hello?" she said breathlessly.

"Hi, Theresa, it's Rick. I've been wanting to call you and not call you at the same time." He paused. "I'm really embarrassed by what happened. I have to admit I'm glad it did happen, but I really had no business .... I should never ..."

He stopped, but Theresa finished the sentence for him.

"Should never have showed honest feeling? Never given in to passion?"

"No, should never have felt desire for another man's wife. And yet I keep wondering if I'll run into you somewhere or how soon the grass will need cutting again. I've been hoping for a little rain to speed up the growing!"

He laughed, and Theresa could picture his smile and the way his blue eyes watched her. She wanted to see him.

"It *is* looking a little long," she teased. "Why not come by this morning? I'll buy you a cup of coffee."

Rick hesitated. He probably did not trust himself, but they had stirred up something that excited Theresa, and she was anxious to be with him. Perhaps he could be pulled from the magnet of his past and entertain new possibilities. She was not sharing his guilt and tingled with anticipation. She felt bold, beautiful, and unwilling to let one intimate encounter be enough.

"I could stop by between deliveries this morning," he said.

"I'll be here," she answered. "Coffee or tea?"

"I'm maxed out on coffee. Tea sounds nice. And Theresa, I found the answer to my question."

She waited, wondering what he was talking about, what question was hanging out there unanswered.

"It's a gerund. Remember? 'A verbal noun ending in -

ing'? I got thrown off track when I got the letter 'n' and assumed the word itself ended in 'ing.' These puzzles are really a tease, just like somebody I know. I can't quite leave them alone."

"I think I'll take that as a compliment." She laughed, relieved that the answered question did not conjure up a barrier between them. "I'll see you soon."

An hour later Rick was at the door. Theresa greeted him in her terry bathrobe. Her hair was still tousled from sleep, but she had taken a long, hot bath after spending the night in her clothes. She smelled of sweet jasmine powder. He held out a brown bag of fresh cinnamon rolls, and the delicious scents combined as she reached for him and they held each other.

There was no waiting, no polite conversation. He did not resist. She led him to the Oriental carpet and slipped off her robe as he lay on her, anxious and ready. The wool nap of the carpet rubbed hard against his knees. She arched to meet him, reaching for the pleasure. They rolled across the clusters of ivory birds and blue patterned vases, and the painted clouds above began to move and swirl with them. Angels nodded, and someone whispered, "yes … yes."

Their clothes were strewn about the floor, but the two lovers showed no interest in retrieving them. Theresa leaned up on her elbow, "Tea time?"

Rick pulled her toward him, their warm, moist skin melting together as one. "You're a bad influence on me, Theresa. But tea sounds great."

She stood up to go to the stove, aware of the eyes following her.

"See," she said, "you should have stuck around at the beach that day I was swimming. You would have gotten the preview."

"Are you kidding?" He laughed, reaching out to touch her. "I was so scared! But you can't imagine how much I wanted to. And then I wondered and fantasized. Theresa, you are so beautiful, but what in the world are we doing?"

"We're having a naked tea party," she answered, handing him a cup of orange herbal tea. "What happened to the cinnamon rolls?"

He reached over and found the bakery bag, handing her a sticky, twisted roll as she sat down on the carpet.

"Sorry these aren't still hot."

"They're perfect," came the reply.

CHAPTER FIFTEEN

The prospect of meeting with Stormy had Theresa's head spinning. She was filled with questions. *How did he meet her grandmother? What was her mother like? Did her grandmother ever go back to South Carolina? And who was Claude?*

The Lobster Pot was an easy restaurant to find. A tired sign lighted by one bare bulb hung out over the sidewalk on the main street, and a steady stream of customers headed through the narrow door, not even stopping to look at the menu in the window.

Theresa found Stormy at a table in the back. She liked the low lights and relaxed atmosphere. It was a perfect place to sit and talk.

"A little chilly to eat outside. What do you think?" he asked, standing awkwardly to pull out a chair for her.

"This is fine. It smells terrific in here. Seafood heaven!"

He wore an old jacket and red plaid shirt with jeans. His face was brown from seasons of sun and harsh weather. He put on glasses to look at the menu.

"I pretty much know this by heart, but I usually order the special, anyhow," he said. "And often I've brought it in! I catch it; they cook it. It's a great arrangement, and there are no dishes to wash. We sometimes work on the barter system here, especially until the tourists pile in; it eases the cash flow."

He laughed, and Theresa gazed at this curious and comfortable man.

"What do you feel like?" he continued, looking down at the menu.

"I feel like sitting here until your voice gives out telling me everything you know about my family."

Stormy smiled at her. "I don't think they'd be open late enough for that."

He ordered two bowls of chowder and two platter specials. Theresa had ventured onto his turf and was very willing to let him guide her through the familiar terrain. He settled back, looking intently at her.

"Where did you meet my grandmother?" she asked. "And when?"

"You're sittin' in her chair," he said simply. "And I've seen that smile a hundred times before, on a different face, across this same table."

Theresa automatically sat upright, startled, suddenly aware that this place was more than a restaurant. It was a fond memory, a shrine to love, a place where two hearts came bare in the shadowy vestibule, away from the light of everyday demands. Like the privacy of her childhood tree house hidden in the high, dense cluster of leaves, this snug table in the back of a busy restaurant provided safety and shelter for an unlikely pair. Theresa waited.

"It was mah-jongg," he said, laughing. "We met over mah-jongg. Have you heard of it?"

She shook her head slightly, eager for the story that was about to come.

"It's a game, an ancient Oriental game, the national game of China. When I was workin' off the coast of Japan as a young man, I bought a mah-jongg set in a local market. The small rectangular pieces are beautiful to see and hold. Mine are made of ivory and bamboo. It's an old set, even when I bought it, and I just liked the feel of the smooth pieces and the interesting Chinese characters and designs. A few have carvings of elegant birds, like heron or peacocks, and there are slim ivory sticks, several inches long, with groups of dots. I had no idea what it was or how to play. My shipmates spent their wages on less permanent pleasures in the village, but I really wanted this old box and its pieces. I felt the hands of history passing their traditions on."

Stormy laughed and continued, "I carried that thing around for several years, often lining up the pieces, matchin' the designs, and wonderin' what in the world it was all about. I knew it was called mah-jongg, but I figured it would always be a mystery to me. Then a boat I was workin' came into Provincetown. As I strolled the streets one evening, I passed a bulletin board of local activities and public events. There it was! 'Mah-jongg Club meets Tuesday at 7:00.'

"With just enough time to clean up and leave the boat in order, I got to the place on the following Tuesday. I lied to my mates that I was meetin' a beautiful woman from town. Little did I know I was fulfillin' my own prophecy.

"With slicked-down hair, clean shirt, and only a couple days' worth of beard stubble, I nervously stepped into the designated room a few minutes after 7:00. The eyes of a dozen women fixed on me. Seated at tables of four, women of all ages were movin' mah-jongg tiles around on soft tablecloths. Their fingers continued to organize the pieces, but their eyes stayed with me.

"I froze in the doorway, my hand unable to let go of the knob. Then the most beautiful girl got up and came toward me. I say 'girl' because she seemed so young, her eyes full of sparkle and welcome. She had beautiful hair, the color of fresh-varnished teakwood shining in the sun. She smiled, and my heart melted. That was Theodosia. She said to come in, and I would have followed her anywhere. Your grandmother captured me that day, as sure as a ship surrenderin' its flag.

"She asked if I was lost, maybe because there were no other men around or maybe because I looked so hesitant. 'Come in,' she insisted before I could get my words together, and so I did. Clutching my mah-jongg set under my arm, I walked behind her toward the table where she had been seated. I felt the assembled ladies accepting this interruption with reserved grace.

"'Do you know how to play?' she asked me, eyeing the box I was carrying. That profound question was the secret of the love I held for her from that day forward. I did not know how to play—not mah-jongg, not cards, not ping-pong, not teasin' or joking, not lettin' down my guard for the simple relaxation and joy of someone's company. She taught me to trust.

"Onboard ship I saw poker games and fights, men losing their valuables over the turn of a card. I was careful and kept separate, buryin' emotion beneath the crusty surface of necessity. I liked life on fishin' boats, the changing seas and new countries. The pay was good, the work hard. A young man with a hunger for adventure and no ties to land or love is eager to follow the horizon. But Theodosia changed all that."

A waitress arrived with bowls of steaming clam chowder and a plastic basket of crackers and hard rolls. Theresa took a crusty roll and broke it open, feeling the soft inside and thinking of Stormy's allusion.

"So did you make a pass at her?" she asked.

He smiled, dumping oyster crackers into his chowder. "Make a pass? I probably couldn't have told you my own name! I felt totally at a loss. 'Man overboard!'"

They sat quietly for a minute, each picturing the events of the story—one rehearsing the facts, the other trying to imagine.

Stormy stared at his chowder, slowly stirring it, and then said aloud, seemingly oblivious of whether or not anyone was there to hear, "It was her nature. It was her nature to make people feel at ease. It was a gift that sprang from her the way the sun can't help shining. Who wouldn't want to bask awhile in that?"

"So did you learn how to play mah-jongg, Stormy? I know you got the girl!"

"Well, I tried. I brought my game along that evening because I didn't know if each player used his own set or how it was done. Turns out the women were pretty interested in my antique ivory set and wanted to know all about where I got it and why I'd bought somethin' I didn't understand. The game pieces they used were made of bone; nowadays they're made of plastic. My presence was accepted that evening because I was the owner of a mah-jongg set—and a superb one—not because I could join in the game. Besides, the tables were all numbered already with four women each.

"Theodosia asked me lots of questions about my life and travels, and I sat right next to her, observing her closely and revealing more of myself than I would have expected. By the end of the evening I had watched the ladies toss dice, change their seats, move, collect, and discard the various mah-jongg pieces. It was rather confusing to me, though I should have liked it for its navigational aspects. East, west, north, and south seating determined the beginning of play.

"Theodosia was mad for mah-jongg! Later, she got the club to come to Chatham for the monthly meetings. And before long, they were all comin' for the whole day and enjoyin' the beach, barbecue dinners at Whimsy Towers, margaritas and mah-jongg late into the night. She liked cultural blending! She taught Emily to play, and sometimes I sat in to complete a foursome, but I'm getting ahead of the tale.

"That first night I was her student. She was a gentle

and coaxing mentor, encouraging me to laugh and open up a bit. But I felt coarse and inadequate, uneducated. She seemed not to notice, however—at least she gave no hint of superiority or dissatisfaction with my ways.

"The club met for only two hours, and Theodosia asked if I'd like to go for a coffee afterwards. Nothin' suggestive or pushy, just friendly. We came here and sat at this very spot. She listened so intently to my stories of the sea and wanted my impressions of everything I had seen. I even confided to her that I liked to draw and had painted a few pictures from my trips."

"Oh, boy!" interjected Theresa. "Now come some clues about all the paintings in the house."

Stormy laughed that wonderful laugh that made his wrinkled face glow with joy.

"We did have some fun! We painted all the time. We had contests with color limitations and size restrictions. We painted on the walls, the furniture, canvas, and paper. When we were alone, we filled the big tub and drew through soapsuds on each other's backs, requirin' the 'painted' one to guess the design."

Still smiling, he said, "Theodosia was really ticklish." He paused. "But now I am an old man, and these are just happy memories. How I loved that woman, even in the last years when she had no idea who I was." His softened voice trailed off. "I just loved her."

Theresa didn't want to interrupt. She was so grateful to hear that this caring man had been with her grandmother during her life and through all the years of her mental decline. *Who could wish for better love than what he had felt for Theodosia?*

"What happened after day one?" she said, finally. "How did you get from this table to the claw-footed tub?"

"One day at a time. She said she would be comin' back to Provincetown the next day and would I like to get together. This happened for a number of days in a row, and I began to think she was makin' up the need for these daily trips. But I didn't object. Back then, of course, I didn't have any transportation, so I was unable to offer to drive anywhere to meet her. She had a beautiful Model T Ford, all shiny and black, and was quite a sight behind the wheel, hair blowin' all directions.

"Well, this went on for three weeks, and she finally admitted that she came only to see me. We just about took over the table that was here and claimed it as our own. We sat and talked until they nearly had to throw us out or sweep the floors around us. She told me all about her marriage and her young daughter at boarding school and how she could not live with a man she did not love.

"At the end of a month, I was scheduled to ship out. Nothing even slightly romantic had passed between us, but I knew I could not leave this woman. I 'jumped ship,' so to speak, and decided to try my luck as my own captain. I bought a small fishing boat with my savings and a bank loan and named her 'Too Late.' Theodosia didn't like the name and wanted to rename her 'Never Too Late,' but I silently cursed your grandfather and knew the woman I was coming to love could never really be mine.

"The rest is a story of friends becoming lovers, inseparable hearts that beat as one—the beautiful, vivacious, Southern firecracker and the ocean-faring fisherman washed in from the sea. Emily was like a daughter to me when she visited her mother, but when your parents came to live at Whimsy Towers, I mostly stayed at my own apartment in Provincetown. I suspect your grandfather knew of me, but we never spoke of him. We pretended we were a family, and I suppose he pretended the same. Polite masks hid the reality."

Stormy finished the last bite of his dinner, and Theresa sat wondering why her father had never mentioned the existence of this man. She feared asking Stormy would hurt his feelings. *Was a family made of flesh and blood or of endearing relationships?* She wanted to draw them all together; she wanted to tell Stormy that she loved him for loving her grandmother.

"Did you stay with Grandmother after my father and I left?"

"Oh, yes. I gave up the apartment that I'd kept for years. We were well beyond appearances at that point, and Theodosia needed me. In many ways those were very happy years for us, quieter years. Fewer parties; less commotion. Ana's baby came soon after—the 'mystery baby,' we called him to ourselves—and we settled in with a different sense of family and routine. I was gone fishin' during the day and sometimes for several days at a time, but I tried to be home early at night."

"What do you mean, 'mystery baby'?"

"Have you met Ana?"

"Not exactly, but I know she still lives nearby and works at the library. I saw her there before I knew who she was."

"She was wonderful with your grandmother—thoughtful, patient, kind—a shy young thing with dark hair and beautiful skin, barely out of her teens. But not many months after you and Tim left, she announced she was expectin' a baby. We were stunned. She never gave a hint of who the father was, and we had never even seen her with a man. Theodosia would not consider losing her, however, so Ana stayed and raised her son at Whimsy Towers.

"The house was once again filled with the joy of a baby, and Theodosia doted on that child, transferring the grief of her loss of you into the happiness of watching him grow. As she began to slip from us mentally, she would confuse him with you and then with her own daughter. I guess a mother is always a mother, giving birth to the desire to nurture. She selected the object of her caring from the confused choices in her mind.

"And that little guy loved her, too. They took endless walks on the beach together, and she read to him and taught him to paint, just like the things she had done with you. He's the one who painted the ceiling in your kitchen. He's an amazing painter, but his real talent is poetry. He loves to write and has quite a way with words, considering."

"Considering what?" she asked.

"He's what you might call 'slow,' not quite natural in his mental development. He had trouble at school, and those were the days when kids like that were called 're-tarded' and left outside of serious education. Ana schooled him at home and never accepted the idea that he couldn't have a normal life."

"What happened to him?"

Stormy laughed. "Happened? Well, he's scrubbin' down my boat at the moment! He works with me takin' out charters, handling the lines and doin' the lifting I can't manage anymore. Claude's my right hand and a fine companion, like he was my own grandson. He's about your age, but simple-like. A good boy."

Another piece to the puzzle had fallen into place. In a curious way, Claude had lived Theresa's life, stepping into her footprints as she disappeared from sight. He'd slept in her bed, read her books, sat in her grandmother's lap. He was the child of attention and focus; she was a memory, kidnapped from the life that went on without her.

She was surprised to feel jealous of this boy, now a grown man, but the feeling was quickly uprooted by re-membering the years of happiness with her father. She knew now that there were numerous stories scattered from the past, and her father had left her to connect the dots. She was gathering glimpses of family history, and Claude was an unrelated relation. They might have grown up like brother and sister.

Over two weeks had passed since Theresa arrived on

Cape. She spoke regularly with Kevin, almost every day, and she liked sharing news of Stormy and Claude and their relationships to her grandmother. The trip was bearing fruit. It was easy to talk with Kevin about all these revelations; a guilty conscience clears quickly when the guilt is not too deep. She had not seen Rick for almost a week, filling her time with Stormy and getting to know Claude.

The young man was shy, at first not wanting even to meet her. But Stormy convinced him to come by Whimsy Towers with his mother, so they could all have dinner together. Theresa marveled at how natural the evening felt. The other three people had lived in her house for over thirty years; they knew its every corner and quirk. She was the present hostess, but really more the true guest.

Each of the visitors sat on a chair or couch with the familiarity of doing it every day. Stormy stretched out his legs on a flowered ottoman and knew just the space to allow for it from the chair. He looked utterly content.

Ana took a little longer to settle in. She had never called back from the message at the library the week before, and Theresa chose not to mention it.

"Thank you for your help with my shell search, Ana. It was very successful. Now that I've met the giver of the sea treasure, we can hear the story firsthand." She looked at Stormy.

In mock irritation, he squirmed and asked, "Is nothin' private from my life with your grandmother?"

"Not if I can squeeze it out of you!" Theresa teased. "I have the feeling this is pretty good stuff, something juicy."

"It's a simple story, really."

Ana looked down, as if she, too, knew what he was about to tell.

"Theresa, your grandmother was incredibly beautiful. She was talented, outgoing, giving, fun, and rich. She was everything I was not and never dreamed of being or being around. And yet here I was. She was older than I was by nearly ten years, but two carefree lovers don't live by the calendar. She wanted me in her life and loved me without a look to the side, but she could never be my wife. Your grandfather was adamant about no divorce.

"I had only my boat and a few belongings in my apartment. I'd lived out of a duffel bag since being on my own as a teenager. Theodosia gave me a sense of belonging and the gift of tenderness and stability. She saw somethin' good in me and pulled it out for all the world to share.

"What could I possibly do for her? Or give her? I could not afford fancy gifts, but I did own one perfect and beautiful thing—a sea shell that I found in the Pacific. Literally found inside a fish. I figured that fish carried the shell around to keep it safe for me, waitin' to offer it up like the Biblical taxes from the fish's mouth. Now I had a need for that shell.

"I wrapped it carefully and gave it to Theodosia on her birthday. I told her I wished it was an engagement ring instead, and for years she referred to it as her 'engagement shell'! I think in a way that was our commitment ceremony, our special marriage. When your grandfather eventually died, Theodosia was not mentally capable of makin' decisions. By then we had been together for many years. Our marriage was settled only in our hearts, and so it really can never be terminated by our parting."

Theresa sat still, thinking over this poignant story and remembering Kevin's gift of white roses in college. She had always thought of them as her "engagement roses." *Could their marriage ever regain that sense of urgent love?*

"Have you always been so romantic?" she asked.

"I've never been romantic. It's just what happens when you love someone and want them to know it."

Ana was nodding her head silently, wistfully, almost as if struggling to keep back tears.

Claude gazed intently at the ceiling, not seeming to follow the story of the seashell.

"Will you tell me about the painting, Claude?" Theresa asked gently. "Tell me how you painted it."

"Ladders. Many ladders," he answered, rocking slightly on the couch. "Many ladders in a row. Hard to reach angels. Hard to find baby."

Theresa stared at the man sitting next to her. His curly hair was not dark like his mother's but a brownish blend of different shades. His face showed no special expression. Ana watched her watching him.

"What baby, Claude? What baby is lost?" Theresa

continued.

"Trees try to tell me. Every day I look for her. The water wants her bad."

Theresa shuddered.

"I'm so sorry," Ana interrupted. "Claude, it's okay. It's okay." She turned to Theresa. "He remembers your grandmother talking of losing her child to the ocean. He wants to find her. He looks for her when he goes fishing with Stormy. Claude hears things in different ways than we do, and he puts thoughts together that do not always make sense. I'm really sorry; he doesn't mean to upset you."

Theresa tried to smile at the sad faces of mother and son, both carrying pain from the past that spilled into the present.

"I understand. It's all right. He actually left me a note at the door about looking for a lost baby. And who is Bobby, Claude?"

Ana laughed, and the mood took a light turn.

"Bobby? Did he write you about Bobby?"

Claude quickly grasped this new topic.

"Bobby here?" he asked.

"No, dear," Ana said gently. "Not just now." She turned to Theresa and continued. "Bobby is a raccoon that started showing up at the house some years ago. He'd sit on the back step while your grandmother had her breakfast on the porch, and before long she had named him and was tossing him her toast. I finally had to sit with her to see where breakfast was headed each morning! She got enormous pleasure from watching him and feeding him, and when she died, Claude continued to leave food. When we moved out of the house, he often came back with scraps. I hope he hasn't troubled you."

Theresa leaned back with a deep sigh of relief. She wanted to ask Claude about being in the boathouse, but she didn't want to upset Ana. It was clear that her secret visitor was an adult child with a lingering love for where he had grown up.

"Oh my, no," she replied. "I'm sure Bobby's grateful for the continued snacks, and no one's left me notes since the eighth grade! I didn't think there was any harm involved. And Claude, I hope to get more notes. Stormy tells me you're quite a poet. May I see some poems sometime?" She waited. "I like to write, too. My father taught me about writing."

As soon as the word 'father' came out, she regretted it and felt embarrassed, but Claude didn't seem to notice. His attention was back at the clouds on the ceiling.

"Cloud boy," was all he said. "Cloud boy." And a happy smile came over his face.

"That's what your grandmother called him," Ana said. "In part, I think, because he painted beautiful clouds—she loved his clouds—and partly because she was getting somewhat confused, and 'Claude' and 'cloud' seemed in-terchangeable. He really adored her, and she him. I think they were able to communicate in a way that none of us could share. They were kindred spirits in an unforgiving world." She looked at her son with deep affection as he stared at the ceiling of swirling clouds and angels.

Theresa had liked Ana at their first meeting but felt this shy woman wasn't quite able to relax around her. Perhaps because Ana had been in charge of this household for so many years and felt turned out, or perhaps she felt disloyal in talking about the past with her employer dead. Ana's tenure had begun at Theresa's departure, so she had no stories to tell about Theresa's family or their times together. The family Ana knew in the house revolved around a fatherless child and a childless couple. She was polite, reserved. Occasionally Theresa caught Ana staring at her, observing her in a comprehensive way, almost analytically.

"I guess I've changed a bit since you last saw me," Theresa offered with a smile. "What's it been? Almost thirty-two years?"

"Yes," said Ana quietly. "You and your father were here for just a few months after I came. It was a difficult time, a time of adjustments. Your father was very distraught, not quite himself, I'm sure." She stopped abruptly, folding her hands in her lap, and then continued, "I made no connection when I saw you at the library until you got out the shell. I'd seen your grandmother hold and rub that shell hundreds of times. It was her touchstone to reality, a concrete link to love when Stormy was at sea. Holding it transported her to a place of safety, to a place where Claude and I could not travel with her."

"Did she seem happy? Was this household ever happy again?" Theresa asked.

"Oh, yes. Theodosia Hampton was not one to be defeated by life. She fought the challenges that lined up at her door, knocking them down with her great energy until she could no longer defend herself. The crowd that gathered became too strong for her. Finally, your father couldn't continue to do battle for himself and her, too. He needed help to be able to move on for your sake, and I was hired as companion. There were many happy years and months at a time when your grandmother was as lucid as you are and sharp as a tack. But occasionally dark clouds crept in without warning."

Ana's eyes wandered up to the ceiling. Beckoning angels with outstretched arms looked down, and Theresa felt an eerie acknowledgement, an unspoken communion. Her breath quickened, and she blurted out, "What happened to her? How did Grandmother die?"

Stormy pulled his feet off the ottoman and sat upright in his chair. He leaned forward on his elbows, cradling his head in his hands. Ana looked toward him, startled, waiting.

"I guess we thought you knew," he said slowly, lifting his face to deliver words that broke his heart. "She gave herself to the sea, Theresa. It was Poseidon's call on a cold night."

Theresa covered her face and burst into tears, heavy sobbing tears of frustration and grief. She felt overwhelmed by events that kept killing her family. Life was no more certain than the turn of a card, she thought—a game of chance decided by the heartless whim of nature's fury.

Stormy continued in a soft voice. "We never dreamed she'd go out in a storm. It was a dark night, angry, loud with lightning and cracking trees. She was often anxious during bad weather, sometimes callin' out for Emily, but she never went outside in it.

"We sat together until she went to bed in her room as usual. In the morning there was no sign of her. We searched the house and then ran desperately to the boathouse. Lying on the dock was one of the life preserver rings from my boat, its faded words 'Too Late' a haunting farewell. Her body was discovered a few days later. Dressed in her nightclothes, she was still clutching your small silver cup in her frozen hand."

Stormy struggled to go on. "We figured she was tryin' to empty the whole ocean to find Em, to keep her safe from the storm. Her little cup was not up to the task demanded by her heart." He tried to smile. "Theodosia never accepted bad odds."

"And my father didn't come back?" Theresa asked, knowing the answer.

"No, we called him, of course, but he said they had already parted. He was a good man, Theresa. He did the best he could, the best he knew how."

"He was full of love," Ana added, thoughtfully. "Gentle and tender. He cared deeply for you and your grandmother but kept a protective wall around himself, like a barrier against hopelessness. He felt so alone without your mother."

Theresa was surprised by such intimacy but got up without comment and hurried over to the oven at the sound of a timer. Dinner was ready, and the strong aroma of spicy lasagna filled the room. She had found fresh oregano and marjoram growing in wild clumps in the garden and made her specialty. She knew the recipe by heart. It was Kevin's favorite dish, and she wished he were there with her.

The four sat at the long, marble-top table, two across from two. Claude rubbed his hand over the carved letters, "TABLE OF THE MUSES," and whispered in a mischievous voice, "My muse says 'apples.'"

"Okay, go on," responded Stormy with a tender smile, and Claude sat up very straight in his chair, not yet taking a bite of his food.

Theresa sat speechless, watching. The young man began, "Cloud boy picks round gifts of sweetness, rosy red the kiss of sun. Fall to ground or climb to pick me, each one special when I come."

Stormy and Ana began to clap and call "Bravo!" Theresa couldn't help but join in, marveling at this spontaneous and creative outburst.

Stormy turned to her. "It's a game your grandmother started at dinner parties. She believed everyone had a muse that provided music or poems or ideas. The table was the place to share them. An equal opportunity table." He laughed. "When your muse spoke to you, you spoke aloud, and if you never offered, Miss Theodosia would call on you to conjure up your inner listening!

"No shrinking violets came to dinner twice! You came, you ate, you opened up! It was always lots of fun, and some pretty good stuff came out. I often thought we should have written some down. We could've had a book, *Madame Whimsy's Round Table of Verse!* Though the table's not round, even those of us who can barely put three sensible words in a row got into the swing of it. And Claude was always included."

The lighted portrait of mother and child peered from the end of the dining room, and Theresa felt a closeness to them that made her feel they would always remain with the survivors of this place—not their spirits, but their spirit. The women in her family didn't give up or give in. She felt she knew them.

CHAPTER SIXTEEN

The phone was ringing as Theresa came up the porch steps carrying groceries. She cursed herself for accepting plastic bags at the store, as she felt the grapes and tomatoes squishing against the jug of milk. Everything collapsed into a jumble as she set the bags on the hanging swing and grabbed the outside phone.

Theresa paused and could not speak. Pushed up close to the kitchen door she saw a large vase of white roses decorated with pink ribbon. The mystery of carrots and notes had finally been settled, but she knew instantly who would send her white roses.

"Hello," she said breathlessly, almost saying Kevin's name.

"Hi, there. I was going to give it just one more ring." It was Rick. "Feel like going out for an intimate, five-course dinner with candlelight and violin players?"

Theresa laughed—still staring at the flowers. "Just one more ring, huh? That's why I don't have an answering machine. I don't want all my gentleman callers thinking it's too easy to find me!" She loved the sound of his voice, relaxed and willing to wander to meet her moods. "And what secret restaurant do you have up your sleeve? Violin players?"

"Well, I was thinking of having the jet brought up and

taking you to New York, or we could just settle for chowder and a burger at the Squire."

Theresa was enjoying his little game. She had no awkward or lonely times with him. She didn't need to rewind conversation and edit out the hurt or the misunderstanding. "Since my sequined dress is at the cleaners, I think it will have to be something local, not too formal."

"Squire's it is. Pick you up at eight?"

"I guess I can slip into a pair of jeans by then!" They both laughed.

A relationship starved for fun will choke and die.

As she hung up the phone, Theresa had to admit she felt stirrings of excitement. Rick made her feel at ease, as if he knew what she was thinking almost before she did. He dared her to be herself and didn't argue with the result. She craved his touch. But for the first time, Theresa felt embarrassed being a married woman rehearsing the desirable qualities of a man not her husband. Whimsy Towers had understanding walls that absorbed indiscretion, but she could not expect Kevin to be so resilient. She knew the clock was ticking.

Gathering up the grocery bags by their stretched-out plastic grips, Theresa headed for the refrigerator, carefully putting the bags on the counter and hoping ice cream wasn't oozing out over the lettuce. As she lifted the cold carton, the sides caved in slightly, and she automatically reached into the drawer for a teaspoon. The spoon ran easily along the soft edges of the melting ice cream, curling like rolling Hawaiian surf. It was cool and pleasing on her tongue—an innocent sensation.

After several bites, she quickly put the groceries away, making a mental note of what was left in the pantry. She imagined her grandmother taking stock of the tall shelves, sealing the tins, and putting colorful labels on the squatty glass jars: tea bags, cocoa mix, dried milk, cinnamon. Many items were left from previous years' use, and Theresa had decided not to throw them out. She pictured Ana closing up the house after Grandmother's death, leaving everything in readiness for the baby who'd grown up far from her inheritance.

Warm days were lengthening now as the season reached toward summer. An erratic breeze sauntered up from the water and caused a slight motion of the wind chimes on the porch, a faint hypnotic sound. Like echoes of vocal chanting tuned to scales in faraway chambers, the music called for meditation. Theresa did not like to think of leaving. She had begun to find her place here, settling in without disturbance.

The vase of roses was like a pair of eyes that found her hiding under a new identity, piercing the comfort of days drawn with fresh strokes and reminding her of unfinished business. She opened the card.

"Next week is a blue moon. Can we try a fresh start? Miss you and love you, Kevin."

Theresa smiled at the thought of Kevin sharing these personal words over the phone for the florist to write. A blue moon had sealed their love physically, but they struggled to keep that closeness in all aspects of marriage.

What did she want—and how willing was she to work for it?

The lilac buds were opening just enough to give hint of the sweet blooms to follow, and Theresa sighed happily at the remembrance of Rick's guarantee. A relaxing bath before he came would feel wonderful, and she put a couple of candles on the porch table before going upstairs, still holding the card from Kevin.

The old tub in the master bedroom bathroom was unlike anything she had ever seen before coming to Whimsy Towers. She chuckled at the thought of "master" bedroom and doubted that her grandmother had ever called it that. The bathtub was huge, a long, narrow, and deep white canoe of a tub, rising from graceful, claw-footed legs. The toenails had been carefully painted bright red, and the short, curved legs were shiny gold. It took a long while to fill, and Theresa tossed a generous cup of bath granules under the roaring faucet.

She dropped her clothes onto the floor and slid into the warm bubbles. Her figure was still good, her skin turning brown from recent days at the beach. Even though she was tall, she could not quite reach the end of the tub with her toes. The fragrant water caressed her as she rolled rhythmically from side to side, her breasts reaching up, as if trying to float to the surface. She stirred the water with her hand and slowly moved her fingertips across her slippery body, exploring beneath the bubbles. She closed her eyes, repeating slowly, "Can we try a fresh start? Can we try a fresh start?"

For a long while Theresa coasted between memories

and longing, lulled by gentle motion, eagerness, perfume, and the promise of moist lilacs.

As the water cooled and the bubbles evaporated, her skin started to feel chilled and bumpy. She reached for one of the large, fluffy pink towels with "Whimsy Towers" stitched in flowing blue letters. There were more than a dozen enormous towels and several terry cloth robes, all embroidered "Whimsy Towers." She tried to imagine a muscular, young Stormy wrapped snugly in pink!

With just the bottom of her hair still wet from the bath, Theresa slipped into her flowered slippers and shuffled to the phone. She knew the number by heart.

"Hello, Rick?"

"Hey. You're not breaking our date, are you?"

Theresa paused for a moment. "Date? Oh, no, of course not. I was just wondering … I'm sure you've had a long day at the garden center. What would you think of just having some Chinese carryout at my place?"

As soon as the question was out, she didn't know whether he'd think she was being transparently forward, foolish, or confused. And she wasn't sure herself.

"That sounds terrific. I'll swing by Ming's on the way. Any special favorites?"

"No, I like them all. Maybe a couple of egg rolls, though."

"Your wish is my command. See you soon."

She hung up the phone and let the towel slip to the floor in front of the mirror. She wondered whether it were easier for older women to stay married, to stay put, to be satisfied. *Would an older body desire a lover?* Her long, sun-tanned legs were a sharp contrast to the white outline of her bikini. If her father could only know how all those years of skating had given her great legs! She turned slowly around in front of the mirror. "Not bad, Theresa Crandall. Not bad!" She laughed aloud and picked up the towel.

An hour later she was just brushing her hair and was finally dressed. She'd tried half a dozen outfits and couldn't seem to match her clothes with her mood. Finally, she settled for a pair of jeans and a knit top with a V-neck collar and long sleeves. It was a mossy green color that almost matched her eyes.

"Anybody home?" came a familiar voice from downstairs.

"Be right there," she answered, her heart pounding a little faster than normal.

"Do you like spicy?" Rick called, as he pulled little white boxes out of a tall bag.

"Surprise me."

For over two weeks, Theresa and Rick had settled into a routine that was both mischievous and caring. They were not greedy, allowing time and space to balance their days and ignite their desire. *Did he belong in that kitchen? Did she?* She smiled and tossed her head as she entered the room, moving toward him and kissing him lightly on the cheek as he held Chinese food in each hand. Neither had mentioned falling in love. Neither dared admit that their behavior had a future or an ending. Theresa wondered at what point Stormy and her grandmother had realized that they needed to be together, to live as if only being together mattered. Grandfather did not get his way and was left behind in the love story that endured. *Obstacles could be stepping stones to happiness.*

Gypsy sat with an expectant look as Rick continued to unpack won-ton soup, spicy beef, and a vegetable dish with chestnuts. As each container was opened for an approving peek, delicious fragrance filled the kitchen, and Rick's stomach growled.

"Theresa, I .... "

"How about we eat outside?" she interrupted, heading to the porch with plates, cups, and chopsticks.

Rick scooped up the cartons of food. She passed him on her way back into the kitchen. "I'll put some water on for tea. Grandmother left lots of choices. Chamomile, lemon, herbal, green, even artichoke! Ever heard of that?"

"I'm yours to experiment on," he teased. "The only requirement is that we both drink the same one. No kings' testers here. Hemlock or nectar of the gods, we share the potion!"

"You are putting yourself dangerously in my hands," she responded, reaching for green tea, but neither of them commented further.

A certain restraint settled over dinner. Rick did not ask about the white roses. Recently he had shown increased eagerness to let go of guilt and reservation, and

Theresa had begun to pull back and resist the temptation of infidelity and deceit. Their roles were switching, and each stumbled in the exercise of changing places.

As night descended around them, the small candles flickered hard to fight off the darkness. Hot wax dripped slowly into patterned clumps on the checkered table-cloth, and Theresa squeezed soft bits between her fingers into odd shapes. She smiled and handed Rick her finger-print in warm wax. Like friends meeting to reminisce, they talked of gardening and cooking, of roads not trav-eled, and choices they had made that defined their lives.

"What's the matter with your marriage, Theresa?" he finally asked her. "We've never really talked about it. Neither of us can pretend it's not a third presence here, the guest that will not leave."

"The matter? How do you mean?"

"Well, obviously if everything was okay, I wouldn't be here, and other things between us could never have hap-pened. Satisfaction doesn't leave an open door. Be hon-est."

She stared at the candle flame as a moth is drawn to light, fixated and helpless. She could not look at him. Tears began to form, but she would not give in to them. She was being required at last to provide words for feel-ings about Kevin she could not explain—or wanted to ignore.

"Sometimes you just don't hang the pictures the same," she said softly.

Rick listened, waiting for her to go on.

"We're like trains going down parallel tracks, but all the blinds are pulled."

"How does that happen?" he asked earnestly, and she knew he did not understand how a relationship could tire. His had not died a slow death.

"Poor communication, impatience with differences, predictability, not enough common ground or joy. It's easier just to shut down."

"But Theresa, that's not a marriage, that's a life sentence!" he blurted out.

She laughed aloud and felt the comfort of companionship that was missing in her life, but the man trying to understand her marriage was not the one in it.

"I guess it's the 'worse' part in 'for better or for worse,'" she replied. And then she added, "Rick, I'm married to a very good man, a nice man. You'd like him. And in a couple of days I must go back to where he is, where we live. We have lots to sort out."

"Are you planning to stay there? What about Whimsy Towers?" He reached across the table to hold her hand, and she did not resist. "And what about me?"

"You fell into my life, and I think it surprised us both. Two hungry puppies ready for love. I feel content and happy when I'm with you, but we both know this is not real. I came looking for answers about family, past and present, not an escape for dishonesty."

"So this was just a respite from responsibility? A spring fling?"

"I think you know better. Hey, you have been the one

with the voice of reason." She laughed and continued, "The one on the high moral ground, remember? I'm just trying to share the view."

"I've slid down the hill!" he responded, still holding her hand and joining the laugh. "Or maybe you pushed me."

Theresa playfully pulled her hand free to open her fortune cookie. As the pieces broke apart, the message glared at her like a face in a mirror: "GOOD CHARAC-TER GUARDS AGAINST TEMPTATION."

CHAPTER SEVENTEEN

The next morning when the phone woke her up, Theresa assumed it was Rick. They had left unresolved emotion hanging like laundry waiting for the sun. Still hoping for an answer that would satisfy them both, neither could quite say goodbye.

"Hi, Theresa, are you available for a beach picnic with the girls and me today? I thought we'd drive over to the site of Marconi's first telegraph."

Theresa laughed. Relief, reprieve. She took a deep breath and realized she didn't have to start the day where night left off.

"Am I calling too early? I didn't want to miss you."

"No, Jeff, it's fine. How are you? How are the girls?"

"We're doing great, thanks. Summer school and day camp start for us in a couple of weeks, but this vacation on the Cape has been like make-believe, just pure pleasure."

Theresa wondered why reality had to be separate from "pure pleasure" and what it takes to pull the two together. Her life seemed to be coming in boxed segments that didn't spill over. She pictured Kevin and Rick and Jeff in large plastic containers, each looking at her through clear walls that held them silent and apart.

"Jeff, I … I don't think I can make it. I'm leaving in a day or so, and I have so much to do."

She didn't sound convincing even to herself.

"Are you sure? Katie and Liz will be so disappointed." Then he added, "We've all looked forward to seeing you again."

Theresa felt a tug at her heart from the two little girls who so effortlessly showed her their affection. She remembered their trusting hands in hers, the ease with which she held them and they had come to help her. She yearned to be part of a family, to be needed by children. She ached for what was not possible with her own husband, yet available with someone else's.

"Jeff, I can't. I just can't."

She knew she was afraid, afraid of false signals and pretending, of wanting fantasy and the mirage of a borrowed life. But just as the distant silhouette of a person gets larger as one approaches it, so the truth was gradually becoming clearer to Theresa. Running away brought her closer to herself. She was ready to go home.

Jeff accepted the finality of her response, and she thanked him for all his help, wishing him well with his own family situation. Then she dialed Kevin. He was just getting into the office.

"Hi, counselor! I need a good lawyer. Got any recommendations?"

Kevin paused, probably unsure where this line of inquiry was headed. Before he could answer, she continued. "I'm just teasing, testing your morning reactions. We're coming home tomorrow, and I'm bringing these gorgeous roses with me. Thank you, Kevin. And I mean it. Will I be in time for the blue moon?"

Gypsy nuzzled her, trying to coax Theresa out of bed. A new day awaited, and there would be fresh smells in the yard to investigate. Exploration and breakfast were the first priority.

"It's been a perfect few weeks. Gypsy has adjusted well here, and she won't like to have her routine interrupted. I think this dog is really your offspring!" Theresa laughed at herself and then added, "Are you ready for us back?"

"Tomorrow? That's a quick exit. Are you running from something?"

She hesitated, readying to twist the words that harbored a lie. Theresa would be bringing home a secret of her own making. "No, there's no running. I came in search of answers, and many questions have been resolved for me. Kevin, I want us to try harder, to have that fresh start. I want us to find the missing link that brought us together. I do miss you."

"I'm liking Whimsy Towers more and more," he joked.

"It's given me a chance to step outside my world and look back on it with clearer eyes. I don't want to lose what we've had. I want us to expand the common ground beneath our feet and not head off in separate directions just to avoid the effort of understanding each other. Love is work and fun and discovery and listening. Can we move our marriage away from indifference?"

Kevin became serious. "I'm willing to try. I want to do better at listening and having fun—really, I do. When you're back, I'm taking a few weeks off to unplug work and focus on what we need to do. Without you, I'd be swallowed by the curse of boredom and monotony." And then he added, "Theresa, could we talk about adoption?"

She felt a fresh start had begun for them both.

CB

A gentle rain began at mid morning, at first cleaning infant leaves and cleansing the air, depriving dust of a place to settle. Gradually the drops grew heavy and pounded on the roof like insistent callers. Theresa carefully closed all the windows and spent her last day on Cape Cod locked in a house of memories brought to light. She tried to remember her first impressions of Whimsy Towers, the shadowy rooms and odd feeling of trespassing.

In a few hours Stormy would be coming to dinner. The rainy day provided plenty of time to pack up things for the trip back to Virginia and to poach a fish Stormy had given her. Venturing quickly down the porch steps, she picked several wet sprigs of parsley from her herb pot. The rain tickled her bare arms. She decided she would leave the pot behind. Part of her was returning home, and part was already home.

Stormy arrived promptly at 7:00. "This is a sad supper in many ways, Theresa. You've left here before, and it's painful all over again."

Theresa hugged the old man, feeling him fragile for

the first time. "I'll be back. I promise I'll be back."

Something in his eyes made her wonder whether he was saying goodbye. He had lived to see the return of Emily's baby, the link to the past that guaranteed the future. Theodosia's legacy was secure for now.

They carried trays of steaming fish and fresh summer green salad up the stairs to the garden room. The large skylight was blanketed with gray. Blotches of rain trickled down the curved glass in eerie designs that disappeared onto the roof. The pounding had lessened, but the storm hung on, leaving the window to the sky unable to provide a view of the declining sun or rising moon.

Around the edges of the skylight, dangling crystal stars caught the light of the room and bounced it among themselves like a secret. Candles flickered.

"I love this room," sighed Theresa, perched happily on a lounge chair with her tray.

"I think it was your grandmother's favorite, too," Stormy replied. "She used to feed the birds right on the window sill and let them fly in to the bird bath. Sometimes your father would be tryin' to write, and somethin' feathery would pass across his face. He'd mumble and shift in his chair, and Emily would laugh so hard he couldn't be upset. The birds especially loved the fountain, and there was no point sittin' in their path. They got real gutsy about it. Territorial."

"Stormy, why the name Whimsy Towers?"

"Do you really have to ask?" He laughed, trying to swallow before getting into another story. "Got a dictionary? This house represented 'out of the ordinary' and 'subject to sudden change.' Those are definitions of whimsical. Its owner was full of fanciful ideas and whims, unpredictable as could be, full of curiosity and fun. She used to laugh that 'whimsy' came between 'whimper' and 'whim-wham' in the dictionary, between whining and the jitters. 'Give me whimsy!' she'd holler, with the fervor of Patrick Henry."

"And the towers? Did she build them?"

"Yes and no. She added the one over her bedroom to match the other side. Nobody knows why the first one was built. Perhaps it was a variation of a 'widow's walk,' an expression Theodosia would not allow. She preferred to think of them as lookouts, not the waiting post for disaster. Hundreds of seamen through history have not returned to anxious loved ones that searched troubled waters for them, and the rooftop widows' walks were well named. The ocean takes what it wants.

"In the days after Emily's accident, your grandmother did stand on her balcony for hours, hoping against the odds. Fixed as stone, staring. But I prefer to remember the years of waving and smiling and throwin' kisses."

"And the colors?"

"You're not a sailor, Theresa! The towers were painted for me—by the Queen of Whimsy. 'Red right return' is the nautical expression. In a harbor the buoy lights are green and red; they guide the captain in. Can you picture which color the right tower is from the water?"

"The red one," answered Theresa, repeating the nautical words to herself.

"Yup. It was your grandmother's way of bringing me back to her, of leading me home. 'Red right return.' Her welcome mat from the water side! When those two towers were lit up on a clear night, I could almost feel her arms reachin' out to me in the beams."

He laughed. "The Coast Guard tried a couple of times to shut her down, but she persisted that she was not manning lighthouses, that they were colored lights on her house for safety. It was not easy to argue with Theodosia! Several times lost sailors did find their way to shore because of her lights, and she'd feed them and let them stay in the boathouse."

"Would you like to live here now, Stormy?" Theresa asked gently.

He closed his eyes but did not speak.

She continued, "You lived here for so long, and I don't know what my plans will be. I think you belong at Whimsy Towers, no matter what happens. I'd like to keep Theodosia's family together."

"She would like that." He smiled, reaching over to put a rough brown hand on her arm. "I'd love to come around when you are here, Theresa. I'd like to meet your husband and see your children run through these rooms, but I could not stay here alone. It's easier to be alone with memories when the walls don't share them."

She did not press him. They finished their dinner in the abandoned garden room and finally said a tearful good night that gathered all the lost years into their embrace.

Before going to bed, Theresa dialed a familiar number. She struggled to speak when the voice answered.

"Hi."

"Hi," came the reply.

"I'm leaving tomorrow."

"I've been expecting this call. I'm trying to understand all this, Theresa, and I didn't want to influence you. I want you to be happy, to live happy. You've reawakened that for me, but I know I cannot hold on to you." He paused. "Good intentions can breed regrettable actions."

"Do you regret our being together?"

"Can I plead the Fifth Amendment? Let's just say I wouldn't change it. But we'll have to leave our behavior on the crowded altar of conscience. Emotions do not always survive, but you've stirred something in me that doesn't want to retreat."

"The right relationship will come," she said, hoping she meant for both of them.

"I ... " he hesitated. "I've taken off my wedding ring. It's the first step in acknowledging the future, that I do have a future. I can still value the past without guilt for feelings I have now, or may have. I thank you for that, Theresa."

"Rick, there is only good in store for you. You're a wonderful man."

The phone was quiet. There was nothing more to be said.

"Will you still look after things for me at the house?"

she asked.

"It'll be my pleasure. You know I love it there."

"Thanks, Rick."

"Goodbye."

Theresa settled back into the pillows on her grand-mother's bed, but sleep would not come. She tried to see the shapes of furniture and paintings, to find the outlines of her now-familiar surroundings, but the room was too dark on the moonless night. The rain had stopped. Nature was still, but she was restless, struggling with shadows of her own making.

"Hey, Gypsy," she called to the dog as she got up and reached for her robe, flipping the switch near her bed. "Let's take a walk."

The startled dog roused quickly, obediently following her mistress down the stairs.

Theresa grabbed a bag of lemon cookies and a raw-hide chew toy and headed out the door. The grass was slippery and cold on her bare feet, but the air was warm and moist, clinging to her with the same insistence that opened tiny buds and made spider webs glisten. Water could draw life slowly into view as well as snatch it cruel-ly away.

Whimsy Towers had stood its guard, a safe haven for Theodosia, a challenge to the wild for Emily. It brought hope to Theresa and a deep breath of new beginnings. She thought of Stormy and his devotion, of Ana with her gentleness and dedicated caring. And sweet Claude, with his curly hair and flair for poetry. She realized that her father, too, had been tempted in this place by the passion of a lonely moment. New life sprang from weakness as well as love. A silent voice told her she had a brother, a secret locked in the history of a shattered family.

For a long while, the two companions sat on the dock munching their snacks. Without a hint of stars or the trickery of moonlight, the thick gray sky wrapped them in hushed belonging. They lingered in the night until the brightness of two colored beams drew them back to the porch, where they slept a deep and peaceful sleep.

ABOUT THE AUTHOR

Ann Hymes is a retired real estate broker and mother of two grown daughters. She has a B.A. in English from Mills College and an M.A. in English from Washington College. Her published work includes creative non-fiction. An active international volunteer, including service in the Peace Corps in the 1960s, Ann lives in St. Michaels, Maryland. Write her at whimsytowers@gmail.com.